Department of Health and
Social Security

Scottish Home and Health Department

Department of Health and Social Services
Northern Ireland

Welsh Office

D1344588

Code of Practice

for the

Prevention of Infection

in Clinical Laboratories

and Post-mortem Rooms

LONDON
HER MAJESTY'S STATIONERY OFFICE

ISBN 0 11 320464 7

PREFACE

There has been pressure in recent years for greater attention to be paid to safety in laboratories, and in particular to the prevention of laboratory-acquired infection. Two events have increased this: the passing of the Health and Safety at Work Act, 1974; and the report of the Working Party into the Laboratory Use of Dangerous Pathogens (the Godber Report), which recommends production of a code of practice for the use of those handling 'Category B' pathogens.

Following the Godber recommendations, a Working Party of expert representatives of those with an interest in laboratory safety was set up in 1975 under the Chairmanship of Sir James Howie. Its terms of reference were 'To produce a code of practice for the prevention of infection in clinical laboratories', including recommendations for safety in post-mortem rooms. This Code is the result of their work.

The Code is based on a draft submitted to the Working Party on the 'Laboratory Use of Dangerous Pathogens' in 1974; and on Public Health Laboratory Service Monograph No. 6 (1977) 'The Prevention of Laboratory Acquired Infection'. The Monograph contains references and explanations which support some of the requirements of this Code.

The Department is setting up an advisory group to keep the Code up-to-date.

CONTENTS

Paragraph   *Page*

Preface   iii
Members of the Working Party   ix

APPLICATION OF THE CODE AND
IDENTIFICATION OF SPECIMENS   1

1   APPLICATION OF THE CODE   1

2   CLASSIFICATION OF MICRO-ORGANISMS, VIRUSES AND
    MATERIALS   1
    a   Category A   1
    b   Category B1   2
    c   Category B2   3
    d   Category C   4

3   INTRODUCTION OF CATEGORY B1 AND B2 MATERIAL
    INTO THE LABORATORY   4

STAFF AND STAFF FACILITIES   5

4   DUTIES OF SAFETY OFFICERS   5

5   TRAINING AND SUPERVISION OF STAFF   6
    a   Graduate and technical staff   6
    b   Domestic services staff   6
    c   Reception and clerical staff   6
    d   Maintenance staff and service engineers   7
    e   Laboratory messengers and porters   7

6   HEALTH OF STAFF   7
    a   Medical fitness   7
    b   Tuberculosis   8
    c   Immunisation   8
    d   Screening tests   8
    e   Pregnancy   9
    f   Medical monitoring   9
    g   Medical and accident records   9

7   PERSONAL PRECAUTIONS   9
    a   Deviation from safety procedures   9
    b   Protective clothing   10
    c   Gloves   10
    d   Protective clothing—Category B1 and B2 organisms,
        viruses and materials   10
    e   Hand washing   11
    f   Food and drink; smoking; cosmetics   11
    g   Cuts and grazes—minor injuries   11

v

Paragraph			*Page*
8	WASHING FACILITIES		11
	a	Handbasins	11
	b	Towels	11
9	REST ROOMS		12
10	CLOTHING ACCOMMODATION		12

ACCOMMODATION AND LABORATORY PROCEDURES

13

11	SPECIAL ACCOMMODATION FOR CATEGORY B1 ORGANISMS, AGENTS AND MATERIALS		13
12	ACCOMMODATION FOR RECEPTION OF SPECIMENS		14
13	LABELLING AND RECEPTION OF 'DANGER OF INFECTION' (B1 AND B2) SPECIMENS		14
14	TAKING OF BLOOD SAMPLES IN THE LABORATORY		14
15	SEPARATION OF SERUM		15
	a	Normal routine work	15
	b	Specimens labelled 'Danger of Infection' (Category B1 and B2)	15
16	RECEPTION AND TRANSFER OF SPECIMENS		16
	a	Specimen containers	16
	b	Internal transport of specimens	16
	c	External transport	16
	d	Distribution of infectious material	16
	e	Transport by air freight	16
17	POSTING PATHOLOGICAL MATERIAL AND CULTURES		17
	a	Improper packing	17
	b	Responsibility for packing	17
	c	Post Office approval	17
	d	Inland post	17
	e	Overseas post	18
	f	Animal pathogens from abroad	19
18	DISPOSAL OF INFECTED MATERIAL		19
	a	Necessity for autoclaving or incineration	19
	b	Laboratory supervision	19
	c	Identification of infected material	20
	d	Containers for autoclaving discarded material	20
	e	Containers for infected waste to be incinerated	20
	f	Containers for hypodermic needles and syringes	20
	g	Containers for broken glass	21
	h	Contents of discard containers with disinfectant	21
	j	Sterilization of infected laboratory material	21
	k	Incineration of infected material	22
	l	Disinfectants	23

Paragraph			*Page*
19	CENTRIFUGES		23
	a	Mechanical safety	23
	b	Infected air-borne particles	23
	c	Centrifugation of Category C micro-organisms, agents and materials	23
	d	Centrifugation of Category B1 and B2 micro-organisms, agents and materials	24
	e	Breakage of tubes in centrifuges	24
20	SHAKERS AND HOMOGENISERS—INFECTIOUS HAZARDS		25
	a	Electrical shakers and homogenizers	25
	b	Tissue grinders	25
21	PIPETTING		25
22	BREAKAGE AND SPILLAGE		26
23	OPENING AMPOULES		26
	SAFETY CABINETS		27
24	BIOLOGICAL SAFETY CABINETS AND LAMINAR FLOW CABINETS		27
	a	Definitions of types of cabinet: limitations of use	27
	b	Exhaust protective cabinets: installation	28
	c	Exhaust protective cabinets: disinfection, testing and maintenance	28
	d	Exhaust protective cabinets: use	29
	INFECTIOUS HAZARDS IN INDIVIDUAL SPECIALITIES		31
25	INFECTIOUS HAZARDS IN CHEMICAL PATHOLOGY		31
	a	Precautions in normal routine work	31
	b	'Danger of Infection' specimens	32
26	INFECTIOUS HAZARDS IN HAEMATOLOGY AND IMMUNOLOGY		32
	a	Precautions in normal routine work	33
	b	'Danger of Infection' specimens	33
27	INFECTIOUS HAZARDS IN MICROBIOLOGY		34
	a	Precautions in normal routine work	34
	b	'Danger of Infection' specimens, Category B1	35
	c	'Danger of Infection' specimens, Category B2	35
28	INFECTIOUS HAZARDS IN ELECTRON MICROSCOPY OF UNFIXED MATERIAL		35
29	INFECTIOUS HAZARDS IN HISTOPATHOLOGY AND CYTOLOGY		36
	a	Precautions in normal routine work	36
	b	'Danger of Infection' specimens	36

Paragraph		Page
30	INFECTION HAZARDS IN POST-MORTEM ROOMS	37
	a Post-mortem room staff and observers	37
	b Techniques	38
	c Accommodation	38
	d Disinfectants	38
	e Equipment	39
	f Anticipation of infectious hazards	40
	g Deaths outside hospitals	40
	h Post-mortems in cases of dangerous infections	40
	j Category A pathogens	43
	k General protection against smallpox	43

APPENDICES

1	Prevention of infection: Model Rules for Domestic Service Staff	45
2	Prevention of infection: Model Rules for Laboratory Reception Staff	47
3	Prevention of infection: Model Rules for Laboratory Office Staff	48
4	Prevention of infection: Model Rules for Laboratory Porters and Messengers	49
5	Preventive inoculation—recommended procedures	51
6	Warning signs	52
7	Leaking specimens—recovering and disposal. Spillage and breakage of specimens and cultures	54
8	Disinfectants for laboratory use	55
9	Testing and disinfecting exhaust protective cabinets	57
10	Disinfecting cryostats	58
11	Protective laboratory clothing	59
12	Post-mortems on patients who have died of viral hepatitis—advice to undertakers and relations	60
13	Opening of Ampoules	62
14	Siting of Safety Cabinets and Room Ventilation	63

SELECTED REFERENCES	69
Index	71

Sir James Howie, LLD, MD, FRCP, FRCPath, Hon FIMLS
(*Chairman*)

C. H. Collins, MBE, FIBiol, FIMLS

H. M. Darlow, BA, MRCS, LRCP, Surg Cdr RN (Ret)

J. M. Dunbar, BSc, MD, FRCPath

T. H. Flewett, MD, FRCPath, MRCP

I. Leighton PhD, FIMLS

G. W. Marsh, MD MRCPath

D. H. Melcher, MA, MB, MRCPath

A. C. Scott, MD, FRCPath

F. Stratton, DSc, MD, FRCP, FRCPath, DPH

J. E. M. Whitehead, MA, MB, FRCPath, Dip Bact

P. Wilding, BSc, PhD, MRCPath, FRIC

J. F. Williams Esq

Post-Mortem Room Sub-Group

W. J. Harrison, MA, DM, MRCPath

A. J. Holley Esq

D. H. Melcher, MA, MB, MRCPath

A. C. Scott, MD, FRCPath

Observers

R. F. Saunders, BSc, MCB, MIBiol, FRIC Welsh Office

A. McIntyre, MB, ChB, DTM & H, DPH, DIH, MFCM,
Scottish Home and Health Department

R. M. Melville, OBE, MB, ChB, DPH, MFCM Scottish Home
and Health Department

D. W. McCreadie, LRCP(Ed), LRCS(Ed), LRST & S(Glas),
PhD, MRCP, MFCM, FHA Scottish Home and Health
Department

A. J. H. Wood Esq Health and Safety Executive

E. J. Morris Esq Health and Safety Executive

Secretaries

Mrs A. D. Johnson (until March 1976)   P. R. Gant Esq

Dr M. A. Buttolph (until July 1976)   Dr Alison Smithies

APPLICATION OF THE CODE AND
IDENTIFICATION OF SPECIMENS

1 APPLICATION OF THE CODE

This Code shall apply to:

a   All laboratories and rooms in clinical laboratories where pathogenic micro-organisms, infectious agents or pathological material are examined, handled or stored.

b   All persons working, under instruction, or visiting any of these laboratories and rooms.

The Code could form the basis, in respect of work activities in laboratories, for a detailed extension of the safety policy that each employer is required to produce under the Health and Safety at Work Act (1974).

c   Parts of the Code may be considered applicable to Health Service practice other than laboratory practice and are commended for study to those concerned.

2 CLASSIFICATION OF MICRO-ORGANISMS, VIRUSES AND MATERIALS

For the purpose of this Code these are classified into 4 groups according to the level of hazard they present and the minimal safety conditions for handling them.

It is accepted that laboratories have no control over the nature of specimens they receive or of the organisms or agents in those specimens. A distinction is therefore made between the occasional isolation and the deliberate introduction of certain pathogens.

a   CATEGORY A. This includes organisms, viruses and materials that are extremely hazardous to laboratory workers and which may cause serious epidemic disease. These require the most stringent conditions for their containment. They are not normally encountered in routine clinical laboratories. Work with them requires the endorsement of the Dangerous Pathogens Advisory Group (DPAG) of the Department of Health and Social Security.* The human pathogens currently listed as Category A by the DPAG are:

> Simian herpes (BO) virus
> Lassa fever virus
> Marburg virus
> Rabies virus
> Smallpox virus
> Crimea (Congo) haemorrhagic fever (HF) virus

---

*The Secretary, Dangerous Pathogens Advisory Group (Section PEH1B) Alexander Fleming House, Elephant and Castle, London SE1 6BY. Telephone: 01-407 5522 Ext: 6860 or 6734.

Machupo HF virus
Junin HF virus
Venezuelan equine encephalitis virus
Ebola virus.

If specimens received in a clinical laboratory are sub-sequently shown to be or are suspected of being infected with a Category A pathogen:

  i All work on those specimens must be stopped and materials, cultures, etc. must be removed to Category B1 accommodation pending transfer to a designated Category A laboratory.

  ii The Medical Officer for Environmental Health must be informed immediately.

  iii All staff who have handled these specimens must be identified and their names and addresses must be made available to the Medical Officer for Environmental Health who will make any arrangements for necessary surveillance.

b CATEGORY B1. This includes organisms, viruses and materials which offer special hazards to laboratory workers and for which special accommodation and conditions for containment must be provided. The human pathogens and hazardous material in this Category are:

  i The following organisms and viruses when work with them involves other than occasional isolation in the routine laboratory:

Bartonella spp.

Brucella spp.

Clostridium botulinum

Francisella tularensis

Mycobacterium tuberculosis and other species of pathogenic mycobacteria

Pseudomonas mallei (the glanders bacillus)

Pseudomonas pseudomallei

Salmonella paratyphi A

Salmonella typhi

Yersinia pestis (the plague bacillus)

Blastomyces dermatitidis

Coccidioides immitis

Cryptococcus neoformans

Histoplasma capsulatum and related species

Paracoccidioides brasiliensis

Chlamydia psittaci

Coxiella burneti and other pathogenic rickettsiae

The causal organism of Legionnaires' disease

2

Arboviruses except Semliki Forest, Uganda S, Langate, Yellow Fever, 17D vaccine strain and Sindbis viruses

Pathogenic Amoebae.

ii All sputum and other material that may contain tubercle bacilli even if examination for them is not requested must be processed in an exhaust protective cabinet in Category B1 accommodation.

iii Materials and reagents known to contain hepatitis B virus used for and during tests for that virus or hepatitis B surface antigen (HB_sAg), i.e. when they are deliberately introduced into the laboratory as test materials and controls.

iv Brain tissue and spinal cord material from patients with Creutzfeldt-Jakob disease and multiple sclerosis when these are subjected to homogenisation or disruption for biochemical and other research purposes (see footnotes 1, 2 and 3).

All specimens that contain or are suspected of containing organisms, viruses and materials in Category B1 must be labelled 'Danger of Infection' (paragraph 13 and Appendix (6)) on both specimen container and request form by the person requesting the investigation.

c CATEGORY B2. Materials in this category require special conditions for containment but do not require special

---

Footnote

1. Evidence available to the Working Party strongly suggests that the Creutzfeldt-Jakob syndrome may be transmissible to man and some experimental animals by parenteral inoculation of brain and some other organs. Attempts to transmit infection experimentally by oral, conjunctival or nasal routes have so far failed. As far as we are aware this hazard has not resulted in cases of this syndrome among neuropathologists and others carrying out research on tissue from patients dying of this disease. The Working Party certainly would not wish to discourage work on such conditions, but in the light of what is now known believe that it would be sensible to take precautions appropriate to Category B2 organisms when handling brain and other tissues (see also paragraph 30 h vii).

2. Reports of an agent transmissible to mice and present in the brains of patients with multiple (disseminated) sclerosis have appeared in recent years, but have not been widely confirmed. It has not been claimed that the agent causes multiple sclerosis. We are not aware of any evidence that pathologists and others working on multiple sclerosis have more frequently contracted the disease than other members of the population. We are, therefore, of the opinion that material from patients with multiple sclerosis need not be handled with precautions other than those appropriate to every clinical specimen. For brain tissue from these, as from other patients, however, Note 3 applies.

3. Several 'new' viruses have been discovered in brain tissue; and there may be others. We therefore recommend that, when large amounts of any unfixed human brain or spinal cord substances are subject to homogenisation or disruption for biochemical and other research purposes, this work must be done under Category B1 conditions and not in the general laboratory.

accommodation. They include:

   i All specimens known to be HB_sAg positive;

   ii All specimens from patients in renal units who have not been screened;

   iii All specimens from patients suffering from infective, or suspected infective, diseases of the liver;

   iv All specimens from patients with defective or altered immunological competence, e.g. with leukaemia or Down's syndrome;

   v All specimens from patients in other 'at risk' groups, e.g. drug addicts;

   vi All specimens from patients suffering from Creutzfeldt-Jakob disease, (except as at 2(b)(iv) above).

  d CATEGORY C. This includes organisms, viruses and materials not listed in Categories A, B1 and B2 above, that offer no special potential hazards to laboratory workers provided that the high standards of microbiological technique and safety required in this Code of Practice are observed.

3 INTRODUCTION OF CATEGORY B1 AND B2 MATERIAL INTO THE LABORATORY

A clear distinction is intended in this Code between Category B1 and Category B2 pathogens and materials that are unknowingly, and those that are deliberately, introduced into the laboratory. It is appreciated that those listed in paragraph 2(b)(i) may be isolated unexpectedly during routine work in ordinary laboratory accommodation. When they are identified they must be transferred, if any further work is required, to the special accommodation described in paragraph 11. Any Category B1 or B2 pathogen or material introduced into the laboratory for research purposes must also be handled in this special accommodation.

Hepatitis B surface antigen (HB_sAg) is included in Category B1 only where tests for its presence are made and when it is therefore deliberately introduced in test materials and controls (paragraph 2(b)(iii)). It is not practicable to require special accommodation for biochemical and haematological tests on specimens from patients who are or who are suspected of being infected with hepatitis B virus, but special precautions are necessary. It is therefore placed in Category B2. These specimens may be handled in the ordinary laboratory provided that the extra precautions described in paragraphs 12, 13, 14, 15, 25, 26, 27 and 29 are observed. This is in agreement with the conclusions of the Advisory Group on Testing for the Presence of Hepatitis B Surface Antigen and its Antibody (Second Report, DHSS 1976).

4

STAFF AND STAFF FACILITIES

4 DUTIES OF SAFETY OFFICERS

a   Responsibility for safety within the laboratory continues to rest with the Head of the Department, who may delegate particular functions and the authority to carry them out to his subordinates including a Safety Officer (Infection).

b   The duties of a Safety Officer, and deputies, must be assigned to individual members of the laboratory staff who must have sufficient training and experience in microbiology to understand the risks of laboratory infections in all clinical laboratory departments and to give advice on the measures necessary to prevent them. The personal responsibilities of the Safety Officer would normally include ensuring that functions described below are properly carried out. Any failure by laboratory staff to follow the set procedures should, in the first instance, be reported to the Head of the Department for his action.

c   The Safety Officer must have personal access to the Head of the Department, and be informed when any new method, procedure, or equipment is adopted.

d   It will be necessary for the Safety Officer to attend courses and seminars, to visit other laboratories, and to have access to books and periodicals so that he may keep himself up-to-date in matters concerning microbiological safety.

e   He must satisfy himself that all new members of the staff have been so instructed that they are aware of infectious hazards and that members of the medical, scientific and technical staff are competent to handle infectious material.

f   He must carry out periodic 'safety audits' on technical methods and apparatus.

g   He must be informed of any accidents or incidents involving possible escape of potentially infected material, even if there has been no personal injury or exposure.

h   In the event of a spillage or breakage involving infectious material he must be responsible for decontamination procedures.

i   He must keep a written record of all such accidents and incidents in case they may be related at a later date to a laboratory infection.

j   He must assume responsibility for microbiological safety when any seminars, lectures, demonstrations or classes are held in the laboratory.

k   He must assume responsibility for the safe disposal of infectious waste (paragraph 18(b)).

l   He must satisfy himself that any apparatus requiring repair or servicing is disinfected if necessary before it is handled by nonlaboratory personnel, who must report to the Safety Officer before attending to any apparatus requiring attention.

m He must liaise with any occupational health service established by the employer for his staff, be accessible to consult with and advise any safety representatives appointed within the laboratory under the Health and Safety at Work Act, and participate where necessary in any safety committees where matters relevant to safety in the laboratory are under discussion.

n He must inform the local Fire Service in advance of any infectious hazard to which firemen may be exposed in the course of their duties.

5 TRAINING AND SUPERVISION OF STAFF

a GRADUATE AND TECHNICAL STAFF

i All members of the medical, scientific and technical staff must have ready access to a copy of the laboratory safety rules and code of practice.

ii Heads of Departments must thereafter satisfy themselves that all individuals who handle micro-organisms, infectious agents and pathological material have received sufficient training for it to be safe for them to do so, and that junior staff are adequately supervised.

b DOMESTIC SERVICES STAFF

i Although cleaning and domestic staff will not normally handle infectious material, the nature and the hazards of the laboratory work and the precautions against infection relevant to their own activities must be explained to them by the Domestic Supervisor and Safety Officer (paragraph 4(e)).

ii The rules about wearing protective clothing and hand-washing; and about not eating, drinking, smoking and applying cosmetics; and about the reporting of accidents must apply to domestic staff. A set of easily understood rules (Appendix 1) must be given to each person and displayed in appropriate places.

iii Precise instructions must be given to cleaning and domestic staff about which areas they may clean, and which they must not (e.g. benches on which pathogens are handled).

iv Cleaning and domestic staff must be warned and trained not to handle any materials or articles on laboratory benches except under supervision.

c RECEPTION AND CLERICAL STAFF

i A clear distinction must be made between reception of specimens and general clerical duties. Untrained staff must not handle specimens and must not be employed in reception areas.

ii Staff receiving specimens must wear protective clothing (paragraph 7(b)(ii)) similar to that worn by laboratory staff. Other rules for the prevention of infection given in this code must apply to them. A set of easily understood rules (Appendix 2) must be given to each member of the reception staff and displayed in the reception area.

iii Reception staff who receive specimens must not be permitted to handle leaking or broken specimens. These must be dealt with by technical staff. (See paragraph 22 and Appendix 7.)

d MAINTENANCE STAFF AND SERVICE ENGINEERS

All maintenance staff and service engineers must be supervised while they are working in the laboratory, must be advised to wash their hands before leaving, and, if necessary must change their clothing.

e LABORATORY MESSENGERS AND PORTERS

i Messengers and porters who collect specimens from wards and departments must be provided with collection trays or boxes of suitable design (paragraph 16(b)(i)). Specimens must not be carried in the hands or in the pockets or taken into canteens or rest rooms.

ii They must wear protective clothing (paragraph 7(b)(ii)). Other rules for the prevention of infection, given in this Code, must apply to them. A set of easily understood rules must be given to each messenger and porter. (Appendix 4).

6 HEALTH OF STAFF

Where the employing authority has an Occupational Health Service for the staff, the administration and application of the measures set out below will normally be undertaken by that service.

a MEDICAL FITNESS

i 'An employee's state of health must be consistent with the employment sought and unlikely to endanger the health of others' (Tunbridge Report*).

ii Before employment a prospective laboratory employee must either have a medical examination by a doctor appointed by the employer or provide a statement from his general medical practitioner that, having regard to the risks involved, he is medically fit for the employment.

iii All such prospective employees must have a large film Chest X-ray or produce evidence of having had one in the previous 12 months. It is important to avoid the taking of more X-ray pictures than are necessary. Persons interviewed

*Central Health Services Council (1968) Report of the Joint Committee on the Care of the Health of Hospital Staff. Chairman: Sir Ronald Tunbridge. London: HMSO.

for several jobs may have had several X-rays. They must be given a note to say where and when they were X-rayed. Employers must accept a recent X-ray report.

b TUBERCULOSIS

 i All staff who handle known or suspected tuberculous material must have an annual large film chest X-ray. Staff not handling known or suspected tuberculous material must be offered chest X-rays at intervals of not more than 3 years.

 ii Before starting employment all staff must have a skin test for tuberculosis or provide evidence of having a positive reaction. Those with negative skin tests must be offered BCG vaccination and be re-tested. They must not handle tuberculous material until they show a positive reaction. Staff who handle tuberculous or potentially tuberculous material must be re-tested at intervals of not more than 5 years.

c IMMUNISATION

 i Each member of the staff must be offered such protective immunisation as may be considered necessary by the medical staff of the laboratory unless there are medical contra-indications, when he or she must be so advised. For ethical reasons and for his information the general medical practitioner of each member of the staff must be consulted before immunisation is begun. A list of recommended procedures is given in Appendix 5.

 ii The employing authority must make an immunisation procedure a condition of employment in a laboratory or part of a laboratory if the nature of the work and the risks to the health of employees and their contacts merit such action. Staff already in post who refuse the appropriate immunisation must accept transfer to other work in order to remove potential risks to their colleagues and their families.

 iii Any member of the staff who wishes to be immunised against any organisms or agent must be given that protection provided that an accepted immunising agent is available and that there are no medical or ethical contra-indications. Any such must be explained to him and he must be referred in writing to his general practitioner or the Occupational Health Service.

 iv A record must be kept of offers of immunisation that are declined.

d SCREENING TESTS

 i Rubella antibody tests must be offered to all female staff of child-bearing age and immunisation offered if the results are negative.

ii Tests for the presence of hepatitis B surface antigen (HB$_s$Ag) must be offered to all members of the staff.

e PREGNANCY

Pregnant women who work with viruses must be tested for antibody to rubella and to cytomegalovirus. A change of duties may be necessary.

f MEDICAL MONITORING

i All laboratory workers must be issued with cards ('Medical Contact Cards') bearing the following information: name, address and telephone numbers (day and night) of their own doctors; of a senior medically qualified person and Safety Officer at their place of employment; and nature of their employment.

ii They must be instructed to carry these cards at all times and to show them to the doctor whom they consult if they are taken ill.

iii The Head of the Department or a person designated by him must keep a record of the name, address, and telephone number of the general medical practitioner of each member of the laboratory staff.

iv If any member of the staff is away sick for more than 3 days without a satisfactory explanation of illness the Safety Officer (Infection) must inform the Head of the Department who must ensure that the general practitioner concerned has been advised of the possibility of laboratory infection.

v If the Safety Officer is informed that a laboratory infection is suspected he must investigate possible means of infection and inform the Head of Laboratory (see Accident Records paragraph 4(g)–(h), and 6(g) (ii).

g MEDICAL AND ACCIDENT RECORDS

i Sickness records, and records of immunisation, chest X-rays, and job-associated injuries must be kept by a designated suitably qualified person or by the employer's Occupational Health Service. These must be passed on to the next employer if appropriate.

ii Accident records (Industrial Injuries Act) must be kept and all injuries, however slight, must be recorded.

7 PERSONAL PRECAUTIONS

a Members of the staff must not deviate from or modify the technical procedures devised for their safety without permission to do so from the Safety Officer.

b PROTECTIVE CLOTHING

  i All members of the staff of whatever grade must at all times when working in the laboratory wear the protective clothing provided.

  ii Protective clothing, gowns, coats, overalls, and aprons must give adequate protection and be of a pattern approved by the Head of Department in consultation with the Safety Officer. Unauthorised modifications must not be made.

  iii Protective clothing must be properly fastened at all times.

  iv A change of protective clothing must readily be available to any person who has or who thinks he has contaminated the clothing he is wearing. A minimum of 6 gowns, coats, etc must be provided for each member of the staff.

  v Protective clothing must be changed at least twice a week.

  vi Protective clothing worn in the laboratory must be taken off before visiting rest rooms, recreation rooms, canteens, libraries, and other parts of the premises including wards. Within the laboratory building or premises a notice banning the wearing of such clothing must be exhibited on the doors of such rooms.

  vii When taken off temporarily protective clothing must be left in the laboratory or working area on the pegs provided for that purpose. It must not be placed in personal lockers, adjacent to normal outer clothing, or where staff may brush against it in the course of other activities.

  viii Special protective clothing must be provided for staff who visit wards and who take blood samples from patients. This clothing must be kept apart from laboratory protective clothing (paragraph 14(c)).

c GLOVES

  i Disposable gloves must be worn for handling blood specimens and materials that are known to contain Category B1 or B2 organisms or are labelled 'Danger of Infection'.

  ii Staff must be advised to wear disposable gloves when blood is handled under conditions when the hands or fingers are likely to be contaminated (e.g. when using the Coulter S machine, paragraph 26(a)(ii)) or if abrasions are present.

d PROTECTIVE CLOTHING—CATEGORY B1 AND B2 ORGANISMS, VIRUSES AND MATERIALS

  i The traditional buttoned-front laboratory coat must not be worn when handling Category B1 and B2 organisms, viruses, and materials. A gown, or a wrap-over coat fastened by press studs must be worn, and the sleeves must be tight at the wrists. (Appendix 11.)

10

ii Gowns and coats must not be worn for more than 2 days and must be discarded into the receptacle provided for autoclaving.

iii When the plasma from an HB$_s$Ag positive donation is being handled, an impervious wrap-around apron reaching from chest to ankles must be worn over the coat or gown. Plastic overshoes or rubber boots must also be worn.

e HAND WASHING

i Staff must be advised to wash their hands often during work periods and always before they leave a working area.

ii Hands must be washed after removing protective clothing and after removing disposable gloves.

f FOOD AND DRINK: SMOKING: COSMETICS

i Food and drink (other than samples submitted for investigation) must not be taken into, or stored in any room where infectious material is handled.

ii Smoking must not be permitted in any laboratory or place where specimens are handled.

iii Cosmetics (other than emollient hand cream used after washing) must *not* be applied in any laboratory or place where specimens are handled.

g CUTS AND GRAZES—MINOR INJURIES

All cuts and grazes on hands or on exposed parts of the body must be covered with waterproof dressings.

8 WASHING FACILITIES

a HANDBASINS

i A handbasin must be fitted preferably near the exit in each workroom, in each reception area, and in each office where specimens and request forms are handled.

ii If 10 or more persons normally work in one room 2 handbasins must be fitted.

iii Handbasins must have biflow faucets (mixer taps) and be operated by wrist levers or foot pedals.

iv Handbasins must not be used for any purpose other than washing hands or other parts of the person.

v Soap dispensers must not be fitted.

b TOWELS

i Paper towels must be provided and discarded after use in suitable receptacles.

ii Single Turkish, huckaback, or roller towels must not be used in any laboratory workroom.

9. REST ROOMS

a   A rest room, recreation room or room where food and drink may be consumed and smoking permitted must be provided in or convenient to the laboratory building.

b   This room must be furnished with enough seating to accommodate all the staff who may be expected to use it at any one time.

c   Facilities must be provided for making tea, etc and for preparing small meals. A sink for washing crockery, etc must be provided. A refrigerator must be fitted and used only for storing food and drink. Food and drink must not be stored in any refrigerator used for specimens, cultures, or chemicals.

10   CLOTHING ACCOMMODATION

a   Lockers or lockable cupboards must be provided for outer clothing, valuables, shopping bags, etc. These must not be sited in any general laboratory. They must be kept in separate rooms not used for any other purpose, or in cloakrooms, or in corridors, provided that they do not obstruct access.

b   Pegs must be provided in laboratory workrooms for protective clothing.

ACCOMMODATION AND LABORATORY PROCEDURES

11 SPECIAL ACCOMMODATION FOR CATEGORY B1 ORGANISMS, AGENTS AND MATERIALS

a   A separate room must be provided for:
i   Handling, processing, or culturing sputum, potentially tuberculous material, and mycobacteria. (In cytology laboratories where there is an adequate safety cabinet, the processing room may be regarded as a separate room.)
ii   Testing sera for the presence of hepatitis B surface antigen;
iii   Work, other than occasional routine isolation with any of the organisms listed as Category B1 in paragraph 2(b).

b   The same room may be used for any or all of these activities including the handling of Category B2 material. To minimize the number of persons exposed to Category B pathogens it should not be used simultaneously for handling Category C organisms.

c   The room must be large enough to accommodate at least 2 persons, i.e. not less than 800 cubic feet. Ideally the room should measure not less than 18 square metres (200 square feet).

d   The door(s) must be locked when the room is not in use. Doors must have glass panels so that the occupants can be seen from outside.

e   At least one Exhaust Protective Cabinet (Class I) must be fitted. This must satisfy BS* and paragraph 24(b) of this Code and the recommendations for siting, installation and use are described in PHLS Monograph No 6 (Extract in Appendix 14).

f   Hand washing facilities (paragraph 8) must be provided.

g   A warning note 'DANGER OF INFECTION' within the international 'BIOHAZARD' symbol must be displayed prominently on the outside of all doors giving immediate access to this accommodation and on exhaust protective cabinets, incubators, refrigerators and other equipment where Category B1 micro-organisms, agents and materials and HB$_s$Ag-positive reagents are handled or stored (Appendix 6).

h   A refrigerator and deep-freezer must be provided so that all Category B1 specimens, materials and reagents are stored in this room and nowhere else.

j   Access to this accommodation must be restricted to persons authorized by the Head of the Department. Clerical, domestic or maintenance staff must not be permitted to enter until the environment has been made safe for the purpose.

---

*This British Standard Specification is in preparation.

13

a   A separate area must be provided for the receipt of specimens. This may be a room or part of a laboratory but must not be part of a clerical office, or in a public corridor. It must be provided with a bench or table with a smooth impervious surface which must be resistant to disinfectants. It must not be carpeted. A handbasin must be provided.

b   Entry must be restricted to authorised staff. Patients and others must deliver specimens through a hatch or across a fixed counter.

c   All specimen containers must be kept upright and where possible be placed in racks. Sufficient racks must be provided to accommodate all specimens. These racks must be autoclavable or able to withstand prolonged exposure to disinfectants. Disposable racks, e.g. of card or expanded polystyrene must be treated as disposable and discarded after use.

d   Disinfectant at use-dilution must be made daily (Appendix 8). Disposable absorbent wiping material must be supplied.

e   Disposable gloves must be available in this area.

13   LABELLING AND RECEPTION OF 'DANGER OF INFECTION' (B1 AND B2) SPECIMENS

The laboratory must issue the following instructions to users and must supply the necessary materials:

a   Immediately after collection a 'Danger of Infection' label must be affixed to the container.

b   The container must then be placed in a plastic bag that is either self-sealing or which may be sealed by tape provided. A 'Danger of Infection' label must be stuck on to the request form. This form must not be placed in the bag with the specimen but it may be placed in an external pocket of that bag. Forms must not be stapled to bags.

c   Specimens labelled 'Danger of Infection' must not be unpacked by reception staff. They must be collected by a member of the medical, scientific or technical staff from the reception area, or delivered unopened by the reception staff to the department that is to process them.

14   TAKING OF BLOOD SAMPLES IN THE LABORATORY

a   Blood must not be taken from any patient or member of the staff in any room used as a laboratory room. Separate accommodation must be provided for this purpose.

b   Blood must not be taken from any person known to be infected with Category B1 or B2 micro-organisms or viruses (paragraphs 2(b), 2(c)) except under medical direction.

c Protective clothing must be provided for specimen collecting. This must be kept separately from laboratory protective clothing (see paragraph 7(b)(viii).

d Needles must be removed from syringes with needle forceps before the blood is discharged into the specimen tube.

e Syringes and needles must be disposed of in accordance with paragraph 18(f).

15 SEPARATION OF SERUM

a NORMAL ROUTINE WORK

   i Properly instructed laboratory staff must be employed for this work.

   ii To prevent splashes and aerosols, good microbiological technique must be observed. Potentially infected fluids, including blood must be pipetted carefully, not poured. Mouth pipetting must be forbidden (paragraph 21(a), (b)).

   iii Pipettes must be discarded and completely submerged in hypochlorite (2·5 per cent Chloros), or some other suitable disinfectant. They must remain in the disinfectant at least overnight before disposal as described in paragraph 18(h).

   iv Discarded specimen tubes containing blood clots, etc must be put in suitable leak-proof containers (with the caps replaced) (paragraph 18(d)(i)) for autoclaving and/or incineration as described in paragraph 18(e). Uncapped tubes and bottles must not be placed in these containers.

   v Hypochlorite (10 per cent Chloros) freshly prepared daily must be provided for dealing with splashes and spillage of blood and serum.

b SPECIMENS LABELLED 'DANGER OF INFECTION' (Category B1 or B2)

   i The instructions for separating sera given above must be observed.

   ii 'Danger of Infection' specimens must be processed singly or in batches separate from other specimens.

   iii Disposable gloves must be worn. Vizors must be provided and staff encouraged to wear them.

   iv Centrifuge tubes must be capped, marked distinctly (e.g. colour coded), and centrifuged in sealed centrifuge buckets.

   v Vials or tubes into which serum or plasma are transferred must be similarly capped and marked, e.g. with a distinctive colour, to signify that they contain 'Danger of Infection' material. (Coloured automatic analyser caps are available commercially.)

a SPECIMEN CONTAINERS

These must be robust and leak-proof.

b INTERNAL TRANSPORT OF SPECIMENS

i Special trays or boxes must be provided for the transport of specimens between wards or departments and laboratories. These must be of metal or plastic and must be leak-proof. They must be able to withstand repeated autoclaving or overnight exposure to disinfectant.

ii These trays or boxes must be fitted with bottle or tube racks. All specimen containers must be carried upright.

iii They must be autoclaved or disinfected (paragraph 18) and cleaned weekly and after any visible leak or spillage.

c EXTERNAL TRANSPORT

i Special transport boxes must be provided. They must be of metal or strong plastic and have a fastenable lid (e.g. food inspectors' sample boxes). They must be able to withstand autoclaving or prolonged immersion in disinfectant.

ii The boxes must bear a warning label, e.g. ' "Danger of Infection", if found, call nearest hospital or police station'.

iii The boxes must be fitted with bottle or tube racks unless used for 24-hour urine and other bulky specimens. All specimen containers must be carried upright.

iv The boxes must be autoclaved or disinfected (paragraph 18) and cleaned weekly and after any visible leak or breakage.

v Any specimen transported by vehicle on a non-regular basis must be packed as if it were to be posted (paragraph 17).

d DISTRIBUTION OF INFECTIOUS MATERIAL

When material infected with Category A or B pathogens is sent to another laboratory a record must be kept of its nature, its destination, the date of despatch, the method of transport, and the name(s) of the person(s) authorising distribution. Where possible the sender must notify the receiver that the packet has been or will be sent and the recipient must promptly acknowledge receipt.

e TRANSPORT BY AIR FREIGHT (SEE ALSO OVERSEAS POST, PARAGRAPH 17(e))

Material containing micro-organisms, viruses or other agents in Categories A, B1, B2 and C must be packed and shipped in accordance with the requirements for Etiologic Agents, of the International Air Transport Association (Restricted Articles Regulations). This is published annually (in English) by the Association whose address is PO Box 160, 1216 Cointrin, Geneva, Switzerland. These regulations are usually available for reference at the offices of air-freight carriers.*

17 POSTING PATHOLOGICAL MATERIAL AND CULTURES

This section has been approved by the Post Office.

a Infected material that is improperly or carelessly packed and which may leak or be broken in transit offers a serious hazard to the health of people who handle the mail and to the recipient of a damaged packet and any other packet which might have become infected. Post Office regulations are quite clear and must be followed at all times.

b Packing for despatch by post (inland or overseas) must be the responsibility of a trained person, e.g. a member of the reception staff. It must not be entrusted to an untrained member of the clerical staff.

c The packing to be used must be approved by the Post Office. Sample packs together with details of the nature and quantities of the contents should be submitted to:—

Postal Headquarters
PMKD/PMk 1.3   (for Inland Post—Telephone
                                               01-432 5161)

POD/PO4.1.2   (for Overseas Post—Telephone
                                               01-532 5178)

St Martin's-le-Grand
LONDON
EC1A 1HQ

A pack is approved for a specific purpose only and must not be used for any other purpose. Copies of Post Office regulations are available from these addresses. The main points are as follows:

d INLAND POST

i Pathological material and cultures of micro-organisms must be sent by First Class Letter Post only. Post Office regulations specifically forbid sending such material by Second Class Letter or Parcel Post. The properly packed article is officially described as a 'packet'.

ii The specimen must be in a securely closed container, which must be robust and leak-proof.

---

*Advice may also be obtained from the British Members of the WHO Group on International Transfer of Research Materials:

Mr W. Bruce, Disease Security Officer, Animal Virus Research Institute, Pirbright, Woking, Surrey GU24 0NF. Telephone Worplesden 2441

Mr C. H. Collins, Regional Tuberculosis Laboratory, Public Health Laboratory, Dulwich Hospital, East Dulwich Grove, London SE22 8QF. Telephone 01-693 2830

Dr R. J. Harris, Director, Microbiological Research Establishment, Porton Down, Salisbury, Wilts SP4 0JC. Telephone 0980 610391.

iii Each specimen container must be placed in a plastic bag and be completely surrounded by a tight cocoon of absorbent material (cellulose wadding, paper tissue, or absorbent cotton wool) to prevent leakage in the event of damage to the container. There must be no glass-to-glass or plastic-to-plastic contact.

iv The packed specimen must be placed in a box or case of suitably strong material such as fibreboard in such a way that it cannot move about. The official NHS-issue board boxes* will be suitable in some cases but the Universal Container box would not be approved for more than one specimen bottle or tube nor would the larger box intended for one 4 oz jar* be approved for more than 4 Universal-Container-size or more than 6 Bijou-bottle size bottles.

v The box or case must be securely fastened and if necessary wrapped or placed in a stout envelope or padded bag. The packet must be marked 'Pathological Specimen, Fragile with Care', and show the name and address of the sender.

vi The District Post Office must be notified at once if any infectious or potentially infectious material arrives in a damaged condition.

vii The sender must be informed if an improperly packed specimen is received.

e OVERSEAS POST

i Pathological material and cultures of micro-organisms must be sent by air mail whenever possible (not by air freight, but see paragraph 16(e)) and must be packed according to the regulations of the Universal Postal Convention. A violet coloured official label bearing the serpent symbol and the words 'Perishable Biological Substance' 'DANGEREUX' must be affixed to the side of the outer wrapping if any. The official labels are obtainable from POD/PO4.1.2. at the address in 17(c).

ii The sender must ascertain from the consignee that the material is acceptable to the postal administration of the country of destination and that the consignee is considered to be a recognized laboratory coming within the provisions of the regulations.

iii All material must be sent in registered letter packets. Other postal services must not be used.

iv All specimens must be packed in a hermetically sealed

*Supplied by DHSS and PHLS Stores.

18

leak-proof inner container of thick glass or plastic wrapped in enough absorbent material to absorb all the contents in case of breakage and placed in a box, itself wrapped in some cotton or spongy material. This box must be placed in an outer box of solid wood or metal with a firmly fastened lid. Special care must be taken in packing substances sensitive to high temperature and packaging must be strong enough to withstand changes in atmospheric pressure during air transmission.

v Approval of the Post Office must be sought for boxes other than those already approved, as issued by PHLS stores.

vi The name and address of both sending and receiving laboratory must be written on the outer wrapping, with the sender's address to the left and at right angles to the consignee's.

f ANIMAL PATHOGENS FROM ABROAD

Legislation affecting the import into Great Britain from abroad of viruses, bacteria and other pathogens of animal origin is currently being revised. The intention is that pathogens which are the cause of the most important animal diseases shall be imported only under licence while allowing greater freedom for others. Pending the promulgation of new legislation, application for a licence should be made in writing to Animal Health Division III, Ministry of Agriculture, Fisheries and Food, Government Buildings, Garrison Lane, Chessington; but in relation to pathogens known or believed to be of relatively minor importance in animal disease control advance professional guidance can be obtained from the MAFF offices at Tolworth (ext no 437). With regard to Northern Ireland, until the legislation is promulgated, applications for licence should continue to be made to Animal Health Division, Department of Agriculture, Upper Newtownards Road, Belfast.

18 DISPOSAL OF INFECTED MATERIAL

a Infected or potentially infected material must be treated by autoclaving or incineration. Infected or potentially infected material must not leave the laboratory unless:

i It has been effectively autoclaved, OR

ii It is in a secure and safe container, and is transported to the incinerator in a safe manner.

b LABORATORY SUPERVISION

i The sterilisation and disposal of all laboratory waste must

19

be supervised by the Safety Officer or another designated member of the staff.

ii Infected Waste to be incinerated must not be placed where the general public have access.

c IDENTIFICATION OF INFECTED MATERIAL

There must be an identification system, e.g. a colour code, for distinguishing between containers for:

i Infected material to be autoclaved.

ii Infected Waste—to be incinerated.

iii Infected 'Sharps', needles, and syringes, which may be autoclaved but which must also be incinerated.

iv Non-infected waste.

d CONTAINERS FOR AUTOCLAVING DISCARDED MATERIAL

i To prevent leakage of infected fluids and contamination of the environment solid bottomed containers with imperforate walls, made of metal or autoclavable plastic, must be provided to receive discarded cultures or other infected material. Wire baskets and other containers that are not leak-proof must not be used.

ii These containers must be further identified externally by Autoclave Test Tape.

iii If autoclavable plastic bags are used they must be supported in these containers and the mouth of the bags turned back over the rim of the container, to ensure maximum steam penetration. Plastic bags to be autoclaved must not be sealed.

iv The containers must be placed in the autoclave without transferring their contents to other containers before autoclaving.

e CONTAINERS FOR INFECTED WASTE TO BE INCINERATED (OTHER THAN 'SHARPS')

i To prevent leakage and contamination of the environment strong 'wet-waste' paper sacks or plastic bags must be provided. The type used in hospitals as 'Infected Waste Containers' are satisfactory.

ii They must be strong enough to prevent puncture by glass, e.g. by pasteur pipettes.

f CONTAINERS FOR HYPODERMIC NEEDLES AND SYRINGES

i Hypodermic needles must be placed in commercially available, clearly identifiable boxes or containers* with imperforate, not readily penetrable walls. When full these must be placed in Infected Waste containers (paragraph

---

*e.g. Metal Box Co. 'Burn Bin'.

18(e)) and incinerated, even if laboratory practice requires that they are first autoclaved.

ii Disposable syringes, placed in one of these containers or in identifiable sacks must be incinerated, even if they are first autoclaved.

g CONTAINERS FOR BROKEN GLASS

All broken glass must be placed in clearly identifiable impermeable containers. If it is thought to be infected it must be autoclaved before disposal, although it may have been in disinfectant.

h CONTENTS OF DISCARD CONTAINERS WITH DISINFECTANT

After overnight contact with infected material the disinfectant in these discard containers must be emptied down a sink through a sieve or colander or a plastic bag with holes in it. Solid matter must then be autoclaved and disposed of as non-infected waste or placed in Infected Waste containers and incinerated.

j STERILISATION OF INFECTED LABORATORY MATERIAL*

    i All cultures and infected material must be autoclaved unless arrangements for incineration that satisfy this Code (paragraph 18(k)) can be made.

    ii Material to be autoclaved must be placed in containers with solid bottoms and sides (paragraph 18(d)). Wire-mesh baskets and containers with holes in their bottoms or sides must not be used for infected articles because infected material may leak between time of discard and autoclaving.

    iii A time and temperature policy must be agreed. *This is usually 121°C for not less than 15 minutes.* (See MRC Report 1959.) The temperature must be achieved in the load. Drain thermometer temperatures must not be accepted as evidence of load temperatures. Timing must begin when the entire load reaches the required temperature.

    iv Thermocouples must be used in autoclaves to ascertain the penetration time, i.e. the time it takes for maximum-load to reach the required temperature. The chamber drain thermometer (dial) will reach this temperature some time before it is achieved in the load.

    v Thermocouples must be placed at the bottom and in the middle of the load.

    vi When the penetration time has been determined for a maximum load this must be added to the required exposure time. This total is the time for a satisfactory cycle (excluding cooling down period) after the thermometer in the chamber drain has reached the required temperature.

---

*Vizors and heat proof gauntlets should be used by staff operating autoclaves.

vii Checks with thermocouples must be done at frequent intervals, e.g. monthly.

viii Autoclave Test Tape must be placed conspicuously across the mouth of the container. This tape indicates by a colour change whether the container with its load has or has not been autoclaved. A 'safe' reading with the tape is not, however, satisfactory evidence that a mixed load of infected specimens and cultures is safe to handle.

ix Autoclave Test Tape is not suitable for placing in the load. Browne's tubes of the appropriate type or similar time–temperature visual indicators must be used. They must be placed in the load, preferably about $\frac{2}{3}$ the depth of the container and accessible or easily seen when the load is removed from the autoclave, e.g. in test tubes or in the fabric sleeves supplied by the manufacturer.

It must be appreciated that a 'safe' reading does not necessarily indicate that sterilising conditions have been achieved. If any load fails to give a 'safe' reading with Browne's tubes or similar indicators after autoclaving it must be regarded as 'not sterile'.

x Incorrect operation is the commonest cause of failure to sterilize a load in an autoclave. If there is repeated failure to sterilise despite correct operation, the autoclave must be examined by an appropriate expert and it must be checked with thermocouples before being allowed for routine use.

xi Browne's tubes and similar indicators must be stored in the laboratory and elsewhere at the temperature recommended by the manufacturers.

xii Spore strips or spore papers must not be relied upon for daily or load-by-load monitoring of autoclaves used for sterilising infected material. They are useful for periodic (e.g. monthly) checks.

k INCINERATION OF INFECTED MATERIAL*

i Incinerators used for the disposal of infected laboratory material must be effectively commissioned and maintained and be fitted with an after-burner or other device to prevent the dispersal of infected particles into the atmosphere by draught or smoke.

ii The Safety Officer must satisfy himself that the incineration of infected laboratory material is adequately supervised.

---

*It is important that where plastic materials are burnt in the hospital incinerator, the proportion between normal waste and the plastic must be limited in accordance with the incinerator's instructions in which as a general rule the plastic content should not exceed 15–20 per cent of the total refuse.

1 DISINFECTANTS

    i There must be a written disinfectant policy, stating which disinfectants are used for what purpose and the use-dilution based on in-use tests for each. Recommendations are given in Appendix 8.

    ii Disinfectants at use-dilutions (Appendix 8) must be placed at each work station for use in case of accidents. These must be changed daily. Use-dilutions must be made fresh each day. Diluted disinfectants must not be stored for longer than 24 hours.

    iii Discard jars, containing disinfectant at use-dilution, must be placed at each work station. The disinfectant must be changed daily and the jars thoroughly cleaned.

    iv Articles placed in discard jars must be totally immersed. The disinfectant must be in contact with all the inner surfaces of the articles and with their contents.

    v Equipment which has been used to contain pathological material or for culturing micro-organisms must not be washed up or disposed of after treatment with disinfectant alone. The one exception is that re-usable pipettes may be washed after not less than 24 hours' total submersion in a suitable disinfectant.

    vi Bulk fluid specimens (e.g. 24 hour urines in plastic containers) that are difficult to autoclave must be disposed of in the laboratory by the laboratory staff as described in paragraph 25(a)(xi) and not in the washing-up area by domestic services staff.

19 CENTRIFUGES—RISKS OF INFECTION TO STAFF

a Mechanical safety is a pre-requisite of microbiological safety in clinical laboratory centrifuges. The current British Standard is being revised and will include specifications for biological safety. The Department of Health and Social Security will advise on suitable models.

b Infected air-borne particles may be ejected when centrifuges are used improperly. These particles travel at speeds too high to be captured and retained if a centrifuge is placed in a traditional exhaust protective or laminar flow cabinet. Good centrifuge technique and sealed centrifuge buckets offer adequate protection from Category B1, B2 and C micro-organisms and agents.

c CENTRIFUGATION OF CATEGORY C MICRO-ORGANISMS, AGENTS AND MATERIALS

The following procedures must be observed.

    i The centrifuge must be operated according to the manufacturer's instructions.

ii Specimen containers to be used in the centrifuge and centrifuge tubes must be made of thick-walled glass or plastic and must be inspected for defects before use.

iii Except in ultra-centrifuges and with small prothrombin tubes a space of at least 2cm must be left between the level of fluid and the rim of each centrifuge tube. Tubes containing infectious material must be capped.

iv Centrifuge buckets and trunnions must be paired by weight, and with tubes in place must be properly balanced.

v To avoid dislodging trunnions and spilling the contents of the tubes the motor must be started slowly and speed increased slowly.

vi Centrifuges must be placed at such a level that workers of less than average height can see into the bowl to place the trunnions correctly in the rotor.

vii Angle heads must not be used for microbiological work except in special high speed centrifuges. With ordinary angle heads some fluid, even from capped tubes, may be ejected because of the geometry of the machine.

viii The interior of centrifuge bowls must be inspected daily for evidence of bad technique, indicated by staining or soiling at the level of the rotor and cleaned if necessary (see also 19(e)(vi)).

d CENTRIFUGATION OF CATEGORY B1 AND B2 MICRO-ORGANISMS, AGENTS AND MATERIALS

The following precautions must be observed, in addition to those described in paragraph 19(c).

i Centrifugation must be done in batches separate from other material.

ii Centrifuge tubes or bottles must have screw caps and must be marked in a way agreed locally to indicate that the contents are in Category B1 or B2.

iii Sealed centrifuge buckets must be used.

iv The sealed buckets must be opened in an exhaust protective cabinet.

e BREAKAGE OF TUBES IN CENTRIFUGES

i If a breakage is known or suspected while the machine is running the motor must be switched off and the machine must not be opened for 30 minutes.

ii If a breakage is discovered after the machine has stopped the lid must be replaced and left closed for 30 minutes.

iii The Safety Officer must be informed.

iv Strong (e.g. thick rubber) gloves, covered if necessary with suitable disposable plastic gloves, must be worn for all

24

subsequent operations. Forceps must be used, or cotton swabs held in forceps to pick up glass debris.

v All broken tubes, glass fragments, buckets, trunnions, and the rotor must be placed in a non-corrosive disinfectant known to be effective against the organisms concerned at use-dilution and left for 24 hours or autoclaved. Unbroken, capped tubes may be placed in disinfectant in a separate container and the contents recovered after 60 minutes.

vi The bowl must be swabbed with the same disinfectant, at appropriate dilution, left overnight and then swabbed again, washed with water and dried. All swabs must be treated as infected waste (paragraph 18(e)). Hypochlorites must not be used: they corrode metals.

vii Sealed buckets containing Category B material must be opened in an exhaust protective cabinet. If a tube has broken the bucket cap must be replaced loosely and the bucket autoclaved.

20 SHAKERS AND HOMOGENISERS—INFECTIOUS HAZARDS

Aerosols containing infected particles may escape from shakers and homogenizers between the cap and the vessel. A pressure builds up in the vessel during operation. Teflon homogenisers are recommended because glass homogenisers may break, releasing infected material and wounding the operator.

a ELECTRICAL SHAKERS AND HOMOGENISERS

i Caps and cups or bottles must be sound and free from flaws or distortion. Caps must be well-fitting and gaskets must be in good condition.

ii Machines must be covered when in use by a transparent plastic casing of strong construction. This must be disinfected after use. Where possible these machines, under their plastic covers, must be operated in an exhaust protective cabinet.

iii After shaking or homogenisation all containers must be opened in an exhaust protective cabinet or fume cupboard.

b TISSUE GRINDERS (GRIFFITH'S TUBES, TEN BROEK GRINDERS)

i These must be held in a wad of absorbent material in a gloved hand when tissues are ground.

ii They must be operated and opened in an exhaust protective cabinet.

21 PIPETTING

a Mouth pipetting must be expressly forbidden in all departments and laboratories.

b Mechanical pipetting devices must be provided and must be used.

22 BREAKAGE AND SPILLAGE

a The Safety Officer must be informed of any major breakage and spillage.

b Broken cultures must be covered with a cloth soaked in a disinfectant. After not less than 10 minutes it must be cleared away using swabs and a dustpan. The broken material and the swabs must be placed in an Infected Waste container (paragraph 18(e)) and the dustpan autoclaved or placed in disinfectant for 24 hours. Disposable gloves must be worn.

c Spilled cultures must be covered with a cloth soaked in disinfectant and left for at least 10 minutes before mopping up with cloths which must then be placed in an Infected Waste container after use.

d If a request form is contaminated the information on it must be copied on another form and the original must be placed in an Infected Waste container.

e Written instructions on dealing with breakage, spillage and leaking specimens must be exhibited in appropriate places (Appendix 7).

23 OPENING AMPOULES

a Opening ampoules may result in dispersion of solid or liquid air-borne infected material. Ampoules containing pathogens must be opened in an exhaust protective cabinet using the method described by the National Collection of Type Cultures and issued by them with cultures (Appendix 13). Ampoules must be held in a wad of tissues to protect the hands when they are opened.

b Ampoules containing infectious material must never be stored in the liquid phase of liquid nitrogen or put there because cracked or imperfectly sealed ampoules may break or explode on removal. If very low temperatures are required they must be stored in the vapour phase only, i.e. above the level of the liquid nitrogen. Whenever possible infectious agents must be stored in mechanical deep-freeze cabinets or on dry-ice rather than in liquid nitrogen.

SAFETY CABINETS

24 Biological safety cabinets and laminar flow cabinets

a DEFINITIONS OF TYPES OF CABINET: LIMITATIONS OF USE

    i *Class I* Open-fronted exhaust protective cabinets. These offer adequate protection to the worker against the inhalation of aerosols containing Category B1 organisms, viruses and materials. This kind of cabinet is usually fitted in hospital microbiological laboratories. The protection offered by these cabinets depends on correct installation and maintenance. (See Appendix 9 and Appendix 14.)

    ii *Class II* Vertical laminar flow cabinets of special design. These recirculate some filtered air, exhaust some to atmosphere and take in replacement air through the open front. There are various designs. All offer protection from contamination to the material handled and some protection to the worker, depending on design and maintenance. They are mainly used in tissue culture work. Until further assessment has been made Class II cabinets must not on any account be used for handling potentially tuberculous material or organisms in Categories A and B1. They may be used for testing for hepatitis B surface antigen, where the risk of inhalation of aerosols is not great and for work with tissue cultures not involving viruses in Categories A and B1. A notice must be displayed on such cabinets forbidding their use for Category A and B1 organisms, agents, and materials.

    iii *Class III* Totally enclosed exhaust protective cabinets which are gas-tight and fitted with glove ports. They are used for handling Category A organisms and viruses when complete isolation of work from worker is required. A high standard of maintenance is essential.

    iv *Horizontal laminar flow cabinets (outflow).* These are designed to protect the work from contamination. A stream of filtered air passes from the rear of the cabinet across the workbench towards the worker. These are NOT safety cabinets and must not be used for handling any pathological materials or cultures of any micro-organisms. They must not be used for mammalian tissue-culture work in clinical laboratories where such tissue cultures may contain viruses other than those with which they have been inoculated. Any aerosols liberated during manipulations are directed at the face of the worker.

    v *Vertical laminar flow cabinets (other than Class II).* Protect

27

the work but not the worker. The risks to the worker are similar to those in (iv) above: infected material is returned unfiltered to the room and may be inhaled.

b EXHAUST PROTECTIVE CABINETS: INSTALLATION

An exhaust protective cabinet (Class I open fronted, paragraph 24(a)(i) above) must be fitted in every microbiological and biochemical laboratory complex, and in every room designated for handling Category B1 micro-organisms, agents and materials. Diagnostic cytology laboratories (other than cytogenetics laboratories) must have access to such a cabinet. This cabinet:

i Must be of a design approved by DHSS and supplied by an approved manufacturer. A British Standard ~~is in preparation.~~ BS 5726: 1979 has been prepared for microbiologi safety cabinets.

ii Must pass through the open face at least 0·75 linear metres per second (150 linear feet per minute) but not more than 1·0 linear metres per second (200 linear feet per minute) of air when tested as described in paragraph 24(c)(ii) and Appendix 9.

iii Must be fitted with at least one High Efficiency Particulate Air (HEPA) filter to BS 3928.

iv Must have an individual exhaust fan fitted at the end of the trunking to maintain a negative pressure in the trunking except where a cabinet exhausts directly to the open air through the wall immediately behind it.

v Must not recirculate air into the same room, corridor, or any other room.

vi Must exhaust to the open air, or via a thimble system* into a total loss (non-recirculating) ventilation system, when:—

1 Non-return valves must be fitted into appropriate branches of the trunking to prevent cabinet air being directed to other rooms in case of fan-failure.*

2 A relay must be fitted, which operates a warning device if the building ventilation system fails.*

vii Must have an airflow indicator which is visible to the worker when he is working at the cabinet face, e.g. the table-tennis ball flow-indicator fitted to PHLS 1970 cabinets.

viii Must be sited as described in Appendix 14.

c EXHAUST PROTECTIVE CABINETS: DISINFECTION, TESTING AND MAINTENANCE

i All exhaust protective cabinets must be washed down after use with a suitable disinfectant. Disposable gloves must be worn for this operation.

---

*A British Standard is in preparation.

28

ii Formaldehyde disinfection, using the method described in Appendix 9, must be carried out weekly and before air grids are cleaned of fluff, filters are changed or any maintenance work is undertaken. A front closure, for use when the cabinet is fumigated, must be provided.

iii The air-flow indicator must be checked daily.

iv The air flow must be tested with a vane anemometer weekly if the cabinet is in daily use and monthly if used less frequently. The method of testing is described in Appendix 9. Testing must be done by the Safety Officer or other designated officer and records must be kept for each cabinet. A cabinet must not be used if the airflow is less than 0·75 linear metres per second (150 linear feet per minute) at any point on the working face.

v The filters must be changed, after formaldehyde disinfection, when the air flow falls below 0·75 linear metres per second (150 linear feet per minute). The primary filter must be changed first, and if the air flow is not restored to this minimum rate the HEPA filter must be changed. Protective clothing and disposable gloves must be worn for handling used filters. Used filters must be placed in suitable bags and incinerated. Filters must be changed by a designated officer or by a manufacturer's service engineer and a record kept for each cabinet.

vi All cabinets must be tested and serviced by a suitably qualified service engineer (e.g. one trained by the manufacturer) at intervals of not less than 6 months. Fans and electrical switch gear may be serviced by local electricians if necessary after disinfection of the system with formaldehyde. The purpose and function of the cabinet must be explained to such electricians.

d EXHAUST PROTECTIVE CABINETS: USE

The use and limitations of cabinets must be explained to all new members of the medical, scientific and technical staff.

i The cabinet must never be used unless the fan is switched on and the air-flow indicator is in the 'safe' position.

ii If it has an openable glass viewing panel, this must not be raised when the cabinet is in use.

iii Apparatus and material in the cabinet during operation must be kept to a minimum.

iv A Bunsen burner must not be used in the cabinet. The thermal head may distort the air flow and the filters may be burned. A microincinerator is permissible, (e.g. Kampff pattern), but disposable plastic loops are preferable.

v All work must be done well inside the cabinet and visible through the glass screen.

vi It must be understood that the cabinet will protect neither the hands nor the worker from gross spillage, breakage or poor technique.

vii The 'night door' of the cabinet must always be closed when the cabinet is not in use.

viii The cabinet fan must be run for at least 5 minutes after completion of work in the cabinet.

INFECTIOUS HAZARDS IN
INDIVIDUAL LABORATORIES

25 INFECTIOUS HAZARDS IN CHEMICAL PATHOLOGY

Hazards arise from contamination of hands, face, and eyes with blood and other pathological material, particularly through splashing, and from ingestion by mouth-pipetting.

a PRECAUTIONS IN NORMAL ROUTINE WORK

   i The precautions and instructions given in other, relevant parts of this Code must be observed.

   ii Discarded pasteur pipettes and pipette tips must be totally immersed in hypochlorite (2·5 per cent Chloros) so that the disinfectant is in contact with all the inner surfaces. They must be left in the disinfectant at least overnight before disposal as described in paragraph 18(h).

   iii Discarded specimens, with the caps in place must be put into suitable containers and autoclaved (paragraph 19(j)) or into identifiable Infected Waste containers for incineration (paragraph 18(e)).

   iv Sample cups and vials must be discarded without splashing their contents or allowing fluid to accumulate in Infectious Waste containers. If they are to be recovered they must be left overnight in strong hypochlorite (2·5 per cent Chloros) before disposal as described in paragraph 18(h) or before washing for re-use. Sample plates must be washed and disinfected daily.

   v At the end of each day the automated system must be washed through with distilled water or the manufacturer's wash fluid to dilute any infectious agent.

   vi Before changing used dialyser membranes the system must be washed through as described above, followed by a wash with strong hypochlorite (2·5 per cent Chloros) for 10 minutes and then more distilled water. The old dialyser membrane must be placed in an Infectious Waste container and incinerated. Disposable gloves must be worn.

   vii The effluents from automated equipment must be discharged directly into the waste water plumbing system or into a sink waste pipe by a long tube inserted to at least 25 cm. Water must flow down the waste pipe while the machine is operating to avoid splashing and the dispersal of aerosols.

   viii About 250 ml of hypochlorite (2·5 per cent Chloros) must be poured down all sinks used for effluents when the day's work is finished, and before any plumbing work is done on the sink and its connections. A warning sign 'Danger of Infection' must be displayed on each sink trap used for effluents. (Appendix 6.)

ix Faeces may contain Category B1, B2 or other pathogens and must be sterilised by autoclaving whenever this is compatible with the tests required. Faeces must not be homogenised in open homogenisers. Homogenisers must not disperse droplets or aerosols into the room. They must be operated, and the vessel opened, in an exhaust protective cabinet.

x Discarded specimens (except 24 hour urines, see below) must be put, with their caps in place, into suitable containers and autoclaved (paragraph 18(j)) or in identifiable Infected Waste containers for incineration (paragraph 18(e)).

xi Twenty-four hour and other bulky urine samples must be disposed of with care. Splashing must be avoided. The sluice must be disinfected at least daily (paragraph 25(a)(viii)).

xii New batches of commercial control sera must not be used unless they have been guaranteed by the supplier to be free from HB$_s$Ag. Locally prepared batches of control sera must be tested for Hepatitis B antigen and confirmed as negative before being put into use.

b 'DANGER OF INFECTION' SPECIMENS

Specimens may be infected with Category B1 and B2 organisms or viruses.

The following precautions must be observed in addition to those described in paragraph 25(a).

i 'Danger of Infection' specimens must be processed by fully trained and qualified staff singly or in batches separate from other specimens, e.g. at the end of a session. They must be clearly marked, e.g. be placed in distinctively coloured cups.

ii Disposable gloves must be worn for filling sample cups and vials. Safety vizors must be provided to protect against conjunctival contamination.

iii When tests are completed and the system has been washed through with water (paragraph 25(a) (v) it must be washed through with hypochlorite (2·5 per cent Chloros) or glutaraldehyde (2 per cent) for 10 minutes and then with more distilled water.

26 INFECTIOUS HAZARDS IN HAEMATOLOGY AND IMMUNOLOGY

Hazards arise from the contamination of hands, face and eyes with blood.

32

a   PRECAUTIONS IN NORMAL ROUTINE WORK

  i The precautions and instructions given in other, relevant parts of this Code must be observed.

  ii A disposable glove must be worn on the hand used for wiping blood from the sample probe of automated equipment. Report forms must not be touched with this gloved hand.

  iii Tissues used for wiping sample probes and for wiping blood from other equipment and surfaces must be placed in Infected Waste containers for incineration (paragraph 18(e)).

  iv Fingers must not be used to occlude tubes containing blood while the contents are mixed.

  v ESR techniques involving mouth-pipetting must not be used.

  vi The method of making blood films must be such that blood does not contaminate the fingers of the operator.

  vii Discarded open tubes, pasteur pipettes etc, must be totally immersed in hypochlorite (2·5 per cent Chloros) so that the disinfectant is in contact with the contents and the whole inner surface. The tubes etc, must be left in the disinfectant at least overnight before disposal as described in paragraph 18(h).

  viii Disposable plastic or glass-ware must be used whenever possible.

  ix Discarded specimens, with the caps in place, must be put into suitable containers and autoclaved (paragraph 18(j)) or into identifiable Infected Waste containers for incineration (paragraph 18(e) (x)).

  x Effluents from automated equipment must be collected in jars for disposal in the same way as 24-hour urines (paragraph 25(a)(xi)) or discharged directly into the waste plumbing (paragraph 25(a) (vii)), by pouring down a sink or sluice.

b   'DANGER OF INFECTION' SPECIMENS

Hepatitis is the most important hazard, but blood may be infected with Category B1 organisms or viruses (see paragraph 2(c) (ii).

The following precautions must be observed in addition to those described in paragraph 26(a).

  i Specimens labelled 'Danger of Infection' must be processed singly or in batches separately from other specimens (e.g. at end of a session), by fully trained and qualified staff.

  ii Disposable gloves must be worn for all operations, including making blood films.

  iii The specimen tube must be placed in another, larger stoppered tube or bottle for roller mixing.

33

iv Tissues used for wiping probes etc, must be placed immediately in an Infected Waste container.

v Automated equipment must be well rinsed through with water followed by hypochlorite and more water after use.

vi The working area must be cleaned down with hypochlorite when the tests are completed. Swabs and gloves must be immersed in hypochlorite overnight before disposal as in paragraph 18(h).

27 INFECTIOUS HAZARDS IN MICROBIOLOGY

Hazards arise from the inhalation of infected air-borne particles that are generated during most normal microbiological procedures, from ingestion of infected material, and from contamination of skin and eyes.

a PRECAUTIONS IN NORMAL ROUTINE WORK

i The precautions and instructions given in other relevant parts of this Code must be observed.

ii Microbiological loops must be completely closed and not more than 6 cm in length.

iii Where there is a risk of infected material spattering in a bunsen flame a micro-incinerator of the Kampff type must be used. Plastic disposable loops are safer.

iv Petri-dish cultures should not be piled so high that they are liable to fall over or be easily knocked over. They must be stored and incubated in petri-dish racks or in baskets wherever practicable. They must not be piled higher than the sides of the racks or baskets.

v Catalase tests must not be done on slides. Tube methods must be used, or cover-glass methods in an exhaust protective cabinet. Catalase tests may also conveniently be performed by touching a microhaematocrit capillary tube loaded with hydrogen peroxide onto the surface of a colony.

vi Discarded specimens and cultures must be placed in solid bottomed containers (paragraph 18(d)) for autoclaving.

vii *Salmonella typhi* must not be used for in use testing of disinfectants.

viii Discarded pipettes, slides, disposable loops and swabs must be totally immersed in suitable disinfectant so that the disinfectant is in contact with the contents and all inner surfaces. The pipettes, etc, must be left in the disinfectant at least overnight before disposal as described in paragraph 18(h).

ix 'Benchkote' or equivalent must be used or working areas must be cleaned down with suitable disinfectant when work is finished. ✳

✳ Laboratory staff are obliged to ensure that working areas are cleaned down with suitable disinfectant as appropriate.

x Mammalian tissue cultures used in clinical laboratories which may contain viruses other than those with which they have been inoculated must not be dispensed or manipulated in outflow laminar-flow cabinets.

b 'DANGER OF INFECTION' SPECIMENS, CATEGORY B1

The following precautions must be observed in addition to those described in paragraph 27(a).

i All sputum specimens (paragraph 2(b)(ii)), all specimens known to contain Category B1 pathogens (paragraph 2(b)) and all cultures known to contain Category B1 pathogens (except when they are unexpectedly isolated in routine work) must be handled and processed in an exhaust protective cabinet in the special accommodation specified in paragraph 11.

ii Testing for HB_sAg must be done in this special accommodation.

iii These specimens and micro-organisms must be handled only by workers designated by the Head Medical Laboratory Scientific Officer and approved by the Head of the Department.

iv Appropriate protective clothing must be worn (paragraph 7(d)) and discarded as described in that paragraph.

v Disposable gloves must be worn.

vi All discarded paper, paper towels, tissues, wrapping and material normally treated as non-infected waste in other circumstances must be placed in Infected Waste containers for incineration.

c 'DANGER OF INFECTION' SPECIMENS, CATEGORY B2

The following precautions must be observed in addition to those described in paragraph 27(a) and (b).

These specimens may be handled in Category B1 accommodation if available (paragraph 3 and 11) but may be processed in other rooms provided that the following precautions are observed:

i For collection, reception and labelling (paragraphs 12, 13, 14).

ii For separation of serum (paragraph 15(b)).

iii For centrifugation (paragraph 19(d)).

28 INFECTIOUS HAZARDS IN ELECTRON MICROSCOPY OF UNFIXED MATERIAL

Most negative stains for viruses and bacteria do not kill them, and so grids prepared for electron microscopy may remain infective. Grids bearing infectious agents must be prepared in the laboratory designated for working with these agents and *not* in the electron microscope laboratory (unless it has been equipped for safe handling of infectious agents). Preparations must be made in exhaust protective cabinets. Before being placed in the microscope, grids must be disinfected by exposure on each side to a tested source of ultra-violet light or, if feasible, disinfected by immersion in 2 per cent glutaraldehyde for 2 minutes. Instruments, e.g. watchmakers' forceps used for handling grids, must be disinfected. To prevent accidental pricks, the points of forceps must be kept sheathed when not in use, e.g. inserted into a rubber bung.

29 INFECTIOUS HAZARDS IN HISTOPATHOLOGY AND CYTOLOGY

Hazards arise from the handling of unfixed specimens in the cutting-up room, in the laboratory and in using the cryostat microtome and the cytocentrifuge.

a PRECAUTIONS IN NORMAL ROUTINE WORK

i The precautions and instructions given in other, relevant parts of this Code must be observed.

ii Large, unfixed specimens must be handled gently to minimize splashing and aerosol formation.

iii Gloves and adequate protective clothing must be worn for handling all unfixed material.

iv Cutting boards and instruments must be immersed in suitable disinfectant after use and before they are cleaned.

v Cryostat microtomes must be disinfected by soaking the removable parts in glutaraldehyde (2 per cent) and by using formaldehyde (Appendix 10). This disinfection is required after sectioning infectious material (Category B1 and B2) and when defrosting for normal maintenance.

vi Unfixed material suspected of being tuberculous, and all sputa, must be processed in an exhaust protective cabinet before cytological examination.

vii Disposable equipment must be used whenever possible for handling unfixed material and after use treated as in paragraph 18(j) (i).

viii Gloves must be worn when loading or unloading unfixed material in the cytocentrifuge. At the end of each day all removable parts of the centrifuge must be placed in suitable disinfectant and left overnight. The bowl of the machine must be swabbed with 2 per cent glutaraldehyde. When available, autoclavable cuvettes must be used.

b 'DANGER OF INFECTION' SPECIMENS

The following precautions must be observed in addition to those described in paragraph 29(a).

i Frozen sections must not be made of unfixed material from:

1 patients infected or thought to be infected with any of the micro-organisms and viruses in Categories A, B1 and B2;

2 known or potentially tuberculous lesions.

ii If the hot formalin/CO_2 microtome method is used for this material the tissues must be prepared, before section, in an exhaust protective cabinet. The operator must wear disposable gloves. Cutting boards and instruments must be disinfected immediately after use.

30 INFECTIOUS HAZARDS IN POST-MORTEM ROOMS

The Head of the Department of Histopathology must take overall responsibility for safety precautions in the post-mortem room and in this he will have the assistance of the post-mortem room technician and the departmental Safety Officer.

a POST-MORTEM ROOM STAFF AND OBSERVERS

    i At post-mortem examinations staff who do not possess the qualification specified in the appropriate Whitley Council agreement must work only under the direct supervision of a pathologist or qualified member of the post-mortem room staff. Every encouragement and facility must be given to staff to obtain the qualification laid down by the Whitley Council.

    ii On commencing employment staff must be instructed about the risks to their health and that of others if strict attention is not given to cleanliness and hygiene at all times. Staff must have an initial skin test for tuberculosis and chest X-ray, and ensure that their tetanus immunisation is up-to-date. Thereafter these must be repeated at the recommended intervals (paragraph 6(a) (b) (c)).

    iii Clean gowns, waterproof aprons, rubber gloves and waterproof boots must be worn by pathologists and attendants when performing a post-mortem examination.

    iv Observers entering the post-mortem room must wear a gown and over-shoes, unless a railed-off spectators' gallery, whose floor is raised well above the level of the post-mortem floor, is provided for students and other visitors.

    v Boots and overshoes must be removed before leaving the post-mortem room.

    vi Cuts or wounds and needle pricks suffered by the staff must be washed well in running water, encouraged to bleed freely and treated with a fresh solution of an appropriate germicide. More serious injuries may require attention at the accident department and a booster dose of tetanus toxoid. All injuries must be reported and recorded in the accident book. Any infection, however minor, following a cut or abrasion must be reported to a doctor.

    vii No smoking, drinking or eating is allowed in the work area. Snacks and smoking must be confined to the rest room,

37

canteen or office; and hands must be washed before leaving the post-mortem room.

b TECHNIQUE

When an organ is roughly handled, squeezed or sprayed with water an invisible spray (aerosol) is created which may contain an infective agent.

    i High pressure water sprays must not be used.

    ii Organs must be removed as gently as possible and sectioned with care.

    iii All saws produce aerosols and must be used with care. Band saws must have an extract hood attachment. Staff using mechanical saws should wear vizors.

    iv Ragged bone edges must be looked for and covered, for example with a towel.

    v If eyes, or skin are splashed they must be washed immediately in running water.

    vi All spillages must be cleaned up immediately.

    vii All swabs, disposable items and material from dissection or cleaned from sink gulleys must be placed in a plastic bag and incinerated daily.

c ACCOMMODATION

    i The post-mortem room and body-storage facilities must be adequate for the workload, both for the hospital and for any additional coroners' work.

    ii A clean changing/office area with adequate lavatory and washing facilities must be available outside the post-mortem room.

    iii Post-mortem tables, dissecting surfaces, floors, gulleys and walls must be constructed of easily cleanable material.

    iv Lighting and ventilation, especially air extraction, must be adequate and air changes must be of the order of 10 air changes per hour. The air flow must never be directly upwards towards the operator's face.

d DISINFECTANTS

The following disinfectants must be provided (paragraph 181 and Appendix 8).

    i A clear soluble phenolic, used at 1–5 per cent.

    ii Hypochlorite (e.g. Chloros) used at 1 per cent (1,000 ppm available chlorine) or 10 per cent (10,000 ppm available chlorine).
Must not be used on metals.

    iii Formalin solution BP (40 per cent formaldehyde) used at 10 per cent (4 per cent formaldehyde).

iv Glutaraldehyde (e.g. Cidex) used at 2 per cent.
All disinfectants must be freshly prepared for use at the appropriate use-dilution. Diluted disinfectants must not be stored.

e EQUIPMENT
    i *Knives and instruments.* These must be washed clean with abundant running water and then decontaminated, e.g. with phenolic disinfectant.
    ii *Suction apparatus (with trap).* If used to remove fluid these must be washed and disinfected as above. Small glass or metal vessels are easiest to keep clean. Disposable syringes and needles must be used for aspirating small volumes of fluid. After use these must be placed in an Infectious Waste container for incineration.
    iii *Post-mortem tables, dissection surfaces, scales, etc.* These must be washed with water to remove visible stains and then rinsed with a freshly diluted phenolic disinfectant (Chloros may be used on non-metallic surfaces).
    iv *Sponges and Swabs.* If these are re-usable items they must be washed with water and soaked in disinfectant after use.
    v *Clothing.* Clean gowns must be used for each post-mortem session. They must be placed in a 'Foul/Infected Material' laundry bag after use.
    vi *Gloves.* Disposable gloves (BS 4005) must fit well and be changed immediately if torn or punctured. Heavy duty gloves must be washed thoroughly in soap or detergent and warm water and rinsed in running water then taken off the hands and immersed for 2 hours in a freshly prepared phenolic disinfectant.
    vii *Waterproof boots and aprons.* These must be worn. The boots must be long enough to reach above the hems of the aprons. Boots and aprons must be rinsed in running water and then in phenolic disinfectant at the end of each dissecting session.
    viii *Vizors.* These must be worn for the post-mortem examinations on certain special risk cases. See paragraph 30(h) (iv) and (vi).
    ix *Telephones, recording equipment, case notes, etc.* In post-mortem rooms telephones must either be of the type that can be used without handling, or gloves must be removed and hands must be washed before they are used. Gloves must also be removed and hands washed before handling such objects as case notes, door handles, and specimen containers. Photographic equipment must be decontaminated if necessary by whatever method is appropriate to the particular apparatus used.

f ANTICIPATION OF INFECTIOUS HAZARDS

Every post-mortem examination should be done on the assumption that there may be a dangerous infection. Nevertheless if mortuary staff and pathologists are forewarned of an infection in a particular case they will take extra care.

    i When the cause of death is a suspected dangerous infection (i.e. caused by a micro-organism or virus in Categories B1 or B2) a warning must be given to protect those who may be handling the body. (See paragraph 30(j) for Category A infections). *This applies whether or not a post-mortem examination is requested.*

    ii Responsibility for issuing a warning must rest with the consultant in charge of the case. In practice nursing staff will be closely involved and so must be aware of the diagnosis or suspected infection.

The mortuary staff must ensure that arrangements exist for them to be notified before the body is brought in. When the mortuary is not staffed a large notice saying 'Danger of Infection' (Appendix 6) must be hung on the appropriate door of the body store.

The body must be labelled clearly with the name of the infection. A label must be attached to the shroud across the chest and an indestructible tag wrapped around the wrist or ankle next to the identification bracelet.

If a post-mortem examination has been requested, the name of the infection should be written clearly on the request form.

    iii Post-mortem request forms must be used in all hospitals. These must include a simple means of indicating suspicion of tuberculosis, hepatitis or other dangerous infections e.g. the 'Danger of Infection' label (paragraph 3(a) and Appendix 6). The request form must be read by the pathologist and mortuary staff before the post-mortem examination is started.

g DEATHS OUTSIDE HOSPITALS

Post-mortem examinations on patients who die outside hospital are undertaken in most hospital mortuaries. The person requesting the examination must be asked to provide the pathologist with any information regarding dangerous infection.

h POST-MORTEMS IN CASES OF DANGEROUS INFECTIONS

    i Undertakers must be informed about all these cases, and these post-mortems must be done at the end of the list.

    ii *Salmonella Infections.* Where death is known or suspected to have been due to salmonella infection care must be taken in washing out and opening the bowel and in washing down and treating with phenolic disinfectant all surfaces, gulleys, drains, soiled linen, aprons, gloves, boots, and instruments. Care must be taken when sewing up after the return of the gut and viscera and when washing the body.

iii *Tuberculosis.* In all known suspected cases of tuberculosis, the following precautions must be observed:

A change into operating gown and trousers must be made before the post-mortem examination.

Ten per cent formalin may be introduced into the lungs after collecting specimens for bacteriology and before beginning the examination.

Handling of these cases must be minimised and splashing and aerosol formation avoided.

As few instruments as possible must be used; and all must be autoclaved at the end of the session.

The post-mortem examination must be performed by as few staff as possible and wherever possible demonstrations must be on fixed specimens.

Infected organs must be left to the final stage to reduce the time of exposure to infection.

Lungs to be retained for further examination by independent medical panels for compensation cases must be immersed in 10 per cent formalin solution, then transferred to a sealable plastic container to await collection. In addition to the routine practice recommended for cleaning equipment and surfaces, gowns must be soaked in phenolic disinfectant overnight, then wrung out with gloved hands and sent for laundering.

iv *Viral Hepatitis.* Post-mortem examinations should not be undertaken unless absolutely necessary in cases of viral hepatitis, hepatitis B antigen (HB_sAg-positive) cases and all haemodialysis cases unless known to be HB_sAg negative. More detailed guidance is given in Appendix 12.

Needle biopsy of the liver, performed after death through skin covered with glutaraldehyde may be of value in deciding whether it is safe to perform an autopsy and may be all that is required.

If a post-mortem examination is imperative:

A complete change into operating-theatre clothing, preferably of the disposable type, must be made before the post-mortem examination.

Full face protection (vizors) must be worn.

Instruments, tables and gulleys must be disinfected with 10 per cent formalin solution immediately after the post-mortem.

It is essential to use 10 per cent formalin solution as the disinfectant in these circumstances because phenolic disinfectants are believed to be less effective against the hepatitis virus group.

v *Anthrax.* A post-mortem examination must normally be avoided where death is known to be due to anthrax. If the examination must be made special care must be taken to avoid body fluids being spilled, splashed or sprayed on to garments, floors and surfaces. All these must be washed clean, treated with a freshly prepared suitable disinfectant for a minimum of 30 minutes and then rinsed with running water. Clothing must be autoclaved before laundering.

vi *Brucellosis; Leptospirosis.* These infections may be transmitted through the conjunctiva as well as by other routes and if *post-mortems* are to be done, vizors must be worn.

vii *Spongeiform encephalopathy* (Creutzfeldt-Jakob Disease). No case of accidental infection among pathologists, MLSOs or mortuary staff has ever been recorded. However, as the disease has been shown to be transmissible (by percutaneous inoculation only) it is sensible to take precautions. Long-sleeved gowns, water-proof aprons, gloves, masks, spectacles or vizors and rubber boots must be worn. The skull and, if necessary, the vertebral column may be opened with a hand or *oscillating* saw (a continuously rotating circular saw must not be used). Special care must be taken not to cut the dura with the saw. If an electric oscillating saw is used, one must be kept for use on these patients only, because it is difficult, if not impossible, to disinfect the motor. Neuropathology centres should keep a separate set of instruments for autopsies on these and other cases of encephalitis.

Autopsy and other instruments must be disinfected after use either by autoclaving at 121° for 1 hour, or by immersion in a suitable disinfectant: 10 per cent hypochlorite solutions (see Appendix 8), iodophors and alcoholic solution of iodine ('tincture of iodine') are suitable; aldehyde disinfectants must not be used. Microtome and other knives may, if preferred, be disinfected by being heated in oil (e.g. liquid paraffin) to 130°C for 1 hour. Heating in oil up to 150° will not affect the temper and although the metal may be discoloured no damage will result.

Formalin used for fixation cannot be relied upon to inactivate the agent; so samples of brain and other tissue must be kept in fixative in sealed containers marked 'Danger of Infection—Creutzfeldt-Jakob'. Frozen and cryostat sections must not be made unless authorised for a specific purpose. Paraffin and nitrocellulose sections must be cut with care because some infectivity may persist in the blocks even after prolonged fixation. Cryostat chambers must be disinfected by painting or swabbing the interior with iodophor.

j CATEGORY A PATHOGENS

　i Post-mortem examinations must not be made (except under conditions approved by the Dangerous Pathogens Advisory Committee) in cases or suspected cases of infection with Category A pathogens (paragraph 2(a)).

　ii Patients with rabies virus infections should have been strictly isolated and patients with any of the other Category A infections will have been confined to infectious diseases hospitals. Special arrangements and precautions are necessary for the handling of the body in the ward, in the mortuary and in the coffin. The reason for these special arrangements should be explained to the relatives and, if appropriate, reference should be made to the advantages of cremation.

　iii During the removal of the body from the isolation ward and thereafter in the mortuary, it is necessary to:

　　wear full protective clothing and footwear, including aprons and rubber boots (this applies to all staff);

　　the body should be placed in a polythene bag, the bag sealed and burial or cremation should take place as soon as possible thereafter;

　　if there is any possibility of delay the polythene bag should be provided with an air valve fitted with a suitable filter. Before placing it in the coffin the bag should be sponged down with white fluid 1 in 40 (BS 2462: 1961 Group WD);

　　the coffin should be prepared as for cremation; all seams should be sealed with pitch;

　　the body should be covered in the coffin with additional disinfectant-soaked tow or sawdust and packed in securely and the lid should be screwed down and sealed all round with pitch or putty;

　　the outside of the coffin should be treated with an appropriate disinfectant;

　　disposable protective clothing should be placed in impermeable plastic bags which should be sealed and incinerated;

　　non-disposable clothing should be placed in suitable bags and autoclaved.

k GENERAL PROTECTION AGAINST SMALLPOX

　i When smallpox is suspected, all personnel who have attended or handled the body and have not been recently vaccinated must be revaccinated immediately.

　ii Protective measures as described above must be taken immediately.

43

iii All the premises where the body has rested or passed through must be fumigated thoroughly.* This may include the repository, post-mortem room, office, waiting room, chapel and all working passages.

*Appendix vi, Memorandum on the Control of Outbreaks of Smallpox, DHSS 1975, London HMSO.

MODEL RULES FOR DOMESTIC SERVICE STAFF
PREVENTION OF INFECTION

1   Always wear the overall provided for your protection and see that it is properly fastened. Keep it apart from your outdoor clothing, not in your locker. Pegs are provided. Do not take your overalls home to wash.

2   Do not wear your overall in the staff room or canteen. Take it off when you leave the laboratory to visit another part of the hospital.

3   Wash your hands often and always before leaving the laboratory or going to the staff room for food and drink or for a smoke. Cover cuts and grazes with waterpoof dressings.

4   Do not eat, drink, smoke, or apply cosmetics in any laboratory. Use the staff room.

5   Do not touch any bottles, tubes or dishes on any of the laboratory benches unless you have been told by the Safety Officer or your Supervisor that it is safe for you to do so.

6   Do not dust or clean any work benches without permission from one of the laboratory staff.

7   If you have an accident of any kind, or knock over or break any bottle, jar, or tube, or piece of equipment, tell the Safety Officer or your Supervisor or one of the laboratory staff at once.

8   Do not attempt to clear up after any accident without permission from a senior member of the laboratory staff. Do not pick up broken glass with your fingers. Use a dust pan and brush. Follow instructions of senior members of staff.

9   Do not enter any room which has the red and yellow Danger of Infection sign on the door until the occupier tells you that it is safe to do so.

10   Do not empty any laboratory discard containers unless a label or an instruction say that you may do so.

IF YOU WORK IN THE WASH-UP ROOM FOLLOW THESE INSTRUCTIONS AS WELL AS THOSE ABOVE:

1   Do not handle or wash any material that comes from the laboratory until it has been sterilised (autoclaved) or one of the laboratory staff or your Supervisor has told you that it is safe.

2   Do not place broken glass in plastic disposal bags. Use the labelled containers provided.

3   Do not work with the autoclave until you have been taught how to do so by your Supervisor and the Safety Officer is satisfied that you are competent to operate it. Follow the written instructions displayed near to it at all times.

If you cut or prick yourself or have any accident which injures you, however slightly, report it to your Supervisor *at once* and see that the Safety Officer records it in the Accident Book. This may save you a lot of trouble later.

If you obey these simple rules you will be as safe as anyone else who works in the hospital, BUT if you are ill tell your doctor where you work and ask him to talk to one of the doctors in the laboratory. If in doubt about anything, ask the Safety Officer.

MODEL RULES FOR LABORATORY RECEPTION STAFF
PREVENTION OF INFECTION

1 Wear your laboratory overall, properly fastened, at all times in the reception room and when visiting laboratories. Keep it apart from your outdoor clothing, not in your locker. Pegs are provided.

2 Never wear your laboratory overall in the staff room, canteen or dining room. If you do you may spread infection.

3 Wash your hands often and always before you leave the reception room. Cover cuts and grazes with water-proof dressings.

4 Never eat, drink, smoke or apply cosmetics in the reception room. You may infect yourself. Go to the staff room.

5 Never lick labels.

6 If a leaking or broken specimen arrives do not touch it or any others in the same box or tray. Ask a member of the medical, scientific or technical staff to deal with it.

7 Do not unpack or remove from its plastic bag any specimen with a 'Danger of Infection' label. These are delivered in this way because there is a risk of hepatitis and other diseases. Refer them to a senior member of the laboratory staff.

8 Keep all the specimens together on the reception bench. Never put them on your desk or anywhere else.

9 Twice each day, e.g. before lunch and when you finish work for the day, wash down the specimen bench with the disinfectant and disposable cloths provided.

10 Do not allow visitors to touch anything on the specimen bench. Keep children out of the reception room. They do not know the rules and may become infected.

If you obey these simple rules you will be as safe as anyone else who works in the hospital, BUT if you are ill tell your doctor where you work and ask him to talk to one of the doctors in the laboratory.

MODEL RULES FOR LABORATORY OFFICE STAFF

PREVENTION OF INFECTION

Much of the work of the laboratory involves handling material that contains germs capable of causing illness. You are not required to touch anything known to be infected but you may accidentally do so and could carry germs to your family and friends. These rules are made to protect you. Therefore:

1. Wear your laboratory overall, properly fastened, at all times in your office and when visiting laboratories. Keep it apart from your outdoor clothing. Do not keep it in your locker. Pegs are provided.

2. Never wear your laboratory overall in the staff room, canteen or dining room. If you do you may spread infection.

3. Never eat, drink, smoke or apply cosmetics in your office. Go to the staff room.

4. Never lick labels or stamps.

5. Always wash your hands before leaving the laboratory and before eating, drinking and smoking. Cover cuts and grazes with water-proof dressings.

If you obey these simple rules you will be as safe as anyone else who works in the hospital, BUT if you are ill tell your doctor where you work and ask him to talk to one of the doctors at the laboratory.

MODEL RULES FOR LABORATORY PORTERS AND MESSENGERS PREVENTION OF INFECTION

1 Wear your overall, properly fastened, whenever you are carrying specimens. Keep it apart from your outdoor clothing, not in your locker. (Pegs are provided.) Never wear your overall in the staff room or canteen. If you do you could spread infection.

2 Cover any cuts or grazes on your hands with a water-proof dressing.

3 Carry all specimens in the trays or boxes provided, not in your hands or in your pockets. Touch specimen containers as little as possible.

4 If you do touch them wash your hands as soon as possible afterwards.

5 Wash your hands *often*—before meal breaks, and at the end of a spell of duty.

6 If a specimen leaks into the tray or box tell the laboratory reception staff and ask them to get it made safe.

7 If you drop and break a specimen do not touch it or clear up the mess. Send someone to the laboratory for help.

8 If you drive a van make sure that you have a bottle of hospital disinfectant and some cotton wool with you. If a specimen leaks in your van, and runs out of the tray or box pour disinfectant over the mess and cover it with cotton wool. Do not mop it up. Drive to the laboratory for help.

9 If you have a break-down or accident do not let anyone touch the specimens unless they come from a hospital and know the rules.

10 Handle specimens packed in boxes gently at all times.

11 Take care when carrying waste or rubbish from the laboratory to the incinerator or rubbish tip. There may be broken glass or needles. If you find these tell the Safety Officer. Special containers are provided for glass, syringes and hypodermic needles.

12 Never eat, drink or smoke when you are carrying specimens, or when you are in any laboratory room.

13 If you cut yourself or have an accident, however small, tell the Safety Officer and see that he enters it in the Accident Book. This may save you trouble later.

14   If you are ill tell your doctor your place of work in case you have caught a germ from the laboratory. Ask him to talk to one of the laboratory doctors.

If you obey these simple rules you will be as safe as anyone else who works in the hospital. Do not be afraid to ask for advice from the laboratory Safety Officer—that is why he is there.

PREVENTIVE INOCULATIONS— RECOMMENDED PROCEDURES

	BOOSTER DOSE
BCG vaccine	see paragraph 6(b) (ii).
Tetanus toxoid	5 yearly and after accidents if infection is possible.
Smallpox vaccine	3 yearly.
Poliovirus vaccine	when commencing work unless given when leaving school. Subsequently as advised by local policy.
Diphtheria FT	3 yearly only if Schick positive.
TABC (or monovalent typhoid) vaccine	3 yearly.
Rubella vaccine (girls)	none.

Any other recognised prophylactic where work of a special nature is done, e.g. with anthrax, plague, typhus, cholera, *botulinum* toxin.

Reference: IMMUNIZATION AGAINST INFECTIOUS DISEASE

Department of Health and Social Security (1972).

WARNING SIGNS

The International Biohazard sign. Colour—Red on Yellow background.

Available sizes:
   wall size, 203 mm × 254 mm
   label, 76 mm × 89 mm
   tape, 25 mm width.
Supplied by Jencons Ltd., Mark Road, Hemel Hempstead, Herts HP2 7DE.

Other or additional words, e.g. 'Infectious Hazard' or 'Danger of Infection' may be added or purchased separately from any sign manufacturer.

LEAKING SPECIMENS—Recovery and Disposal

Advice must be sought from the Safety Officer before attempting to recover leaking or broken Category B1 or B2 specimens or any specimens labelled 'Danger of Infection'.

To recover other specimens, if they cannot be repeated:

1 Wear disposable gloves. Place container or specimen on a tray and take it to an exhaust protective cabinet. Remove lid or cap and transfer the remaining part of the specimen to another sterile container with a pasteur pipette.

2 Replace cap and place soiled container in a plastic bag and leave it on the tray.

3 If the request form is soiled place it in another plastic bag and place it on the tray so that another person can copy the information.

4 Place the tray in another bag or container for autoclaving, or place the bags containing the original container and form in the appropriate laboratory discard receptacle and disinfect the tray.

5 Repeat this procedure with any other specimen containers that have been contaminated by the leaking specimen.

6 Disinfect or sterilise the tray or box in which these specimens were delivered to the laboratory.

SPILLAGE AND BREAKAGE OF SPECIMENS AND CULTURES

1 Cover spill or debris with germicidal powder.

2 Leave for 10–15 minutes.

3 Put on disposable gloves and sweep cloth and debris into a suitable container, e.g. plastic bag or box using more disposable cloths or paper towels or a strong piece of card. Do not use dust pans and brushes unless these can be autoclaved or disinfected.

4 Place all debris and materials used in the appropriate laboratory discard receptacle.

5 Swab area with routine bench disinfectant.

CONTAMINATED REQUEST FORMS

1 Wear disposable gloves for handling contaminated forms.

2 Dictate information on form to a colleague who will complete a new form.

3 Discard the contaminated form in an Infected Waste Container.

DISINFECTANTS RECOMMENDED FOR LABORATORY USE

GENERAL RULES:

1   Use clear phenolics for most organic matter, tuberculous material and general bacteriology, but not for blood and viruses.
2   Use hypochlorites for minimal organic matter, small amounts of blood, and viruses but not for tuberculous material or metals.
3   Use aldehydes for special purposes only.
4   Wear disposable gloves when swabbing with any disinfectant.

1   CLEAR PHENOLICS

e.g. *Clearsol, Hycolin, Printol, Stericol, Sudol*

These are not much inactivated by organic matter and do not attack metals. They have a wide range of activity, are suitable for tuberculous materials but not for viruses or HB_sAg. They should be used in general microbiology, for discard jars etc, and disinfecting benches. Use all phenolics at the manufacturer's recommended use-dilutions. Do not store diluted disinfectants.

2   HYPOCHLORITES

Chloros, Domestos, Diversol BX

These are considerably inactivated by organic matter and attack metals to varying degrees (Diversol BX is said to be non-corrosive). They are suitable for blood and viruses including HB_sAg, but not for tuberculous material and must not be used for centrifuges, moving parts of machinery or metal surfaces. They may be used in virology, haematology and chemical pathology for discard and pipette jars and surface disinfection. The commercial products usually contain ~~10,000 ppm~~ 100,000 of available chlorine and should be used as follows:

> *General use:* 1 per cent dilution containing 1,000 ppm available chlorine
>
> *For pipette jars* 2·5 per cent dilution containing 2,500 ppm available chlorine
>
> *For blood spillage, etc* 10 per cent dilution containing 10,000 ppm available chlorine

Hypochlorites are compatible with anionic and nonionic but not with cationic detergents.

3   ALDEHYDES

Formaldehyde (supplied as formalin, a 40 per cent solution). *Glutaraldehyde*, e.g. Cidex, Tego-Dor, Tego-Fectol.

Formaldehyde gas and formalin are too irritant for general purposes. Formaldehyde requires a high humidity to be active and is used in laboratories mainly for disinfecting by boiling together equal volumes of formalin and water.

Glutaraldehyde (Cidex) does not readily penetrate organic matter and should be used only on clean surfaces. It is less irritating than formalin. It is useful in virology, for HB_sAg and for disinfecting centrifuges and cryostats. For use it is diluted 2–3 per cent, with 0·3 per cent bicarbonate buffer, as it is most efficient at pH 7·0–8·0. It must be discarded after 12 hours as it deteriorates once made alkaline.

4 GERMICIDAL POWDER

FICHLOR Clearon is a chlorinated iso-cyanuric acid derivative with a wide range of activity, including viruses (but not mycobacteria) and is manufactured by Fisons Limited, Agrochemical Division, Hauxton, Cambridge. It is most useful for gross spillage.

5 DISINFECTION OF ROOMS

Full information is given in the Memorandum on the Control of Outbreaks of Smallpox, DHSS (1975). London: HMSO.

6 DISINFECTION OF CABINETS, FUME CUPBOARDS AND CRYOSTATS

Methods are given in Appendix 9 (Exhaust Protective Cabinets and Fume Cupboards) and in Appendix 10 (Cryostats).

7 DEFINITIONS—USE-DILUTION AND IN-USE TESTS

Use-Dilution. This is the dilution, e.g. in water, at which a particular disinfectant is to be used under laboratory conditions for a particular purpose. It is usually suggested by the manufacturer and is determined by the Kelsey-Sykes Capacity test in specialised laboratories. Reference is made to this test by Kelsey and Maurer (1972). *See* Selected References in this Code.

In-Use Test. The disinfectant is tested while in use for the presence and numbers of living organisms. The method is described by Kelsey and Maurer (1972). *See* Selected References in this Code.

TESTING AND DISINFECTING EXHAUST PROTECTIVE CABINETS (CLASS 1)

TESTING

1 Check air-flow indicator daily. If this does not record a safe air-flow check with anemometer.

2 Check air-flow at working face at least monthly with a vane anemometer. Take 5 readings in the positions marked X in diagram:

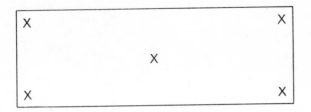

The air-flow at each of these 5 positions must not be less than 0·75 linear metres per second (150 linear feet per minute).

DISINFECTION WITH FORMALDEHYDE

1 METHOD (A) Place 35 ml of formalin BP in a dish on an electric heater in the cabinet. Replace the front closure.* Switch on and boil away the formalin mixture. (Thermostatic control and a time switch are useful.)

METHOD (B) Place 25 ml of formalin BP in a 500 ml beaker in the cabinet. Add 10 g of potassium permanganate and replace the front closure.* The mixture will boil in a few minutes, releasing formaldehyde.

CAUTION If too much potassium permanganate is added there is a risk of explosion. If too much formalin is used, polymer may be deposited in the cabinet and filters.

2 Leave overnight.

3 Switch on the fan and open the front closure a few millimetres to allow air to enter and remaining formaldehyde to be exhausted outside the building.

4 Remove the front closure or open the sash and test the air-flow.

---

*If no manufacturer's front closure is provided make one of hardboard or plywood and attach it over the working face with adhesive tape.

DISINFECTING CRYOSTATS

1 Bring the machine to room temperature.

2 Place 50–100 ml of formalin BP in a flat dish in the cabinet. Replace the front closure.

3 Leave for at least 24 and preferably for 48 hours. Open front closure and place a beaker containing 10 ml of ammonia SG.880 in the chamber. Replace front closure and leave for 1 hour before preparing for use.

LABORATORY PROTECTIVE CLOTHING

OUTLINE SPECIFICATION FOR LABORATORY COAT

1 The design is based on that of Dowsett and Heggie (1972).*
2 Made of white polyester cotton.
3 Wrap over or wrap round to give double front.
4 Side fastening with quick release press studs ('poppers').
5 High neck.
6 Long sleeves.
7 Cuffs to be close-fitting around wrists, for example by ribbed woven material.

---

*Dowsett, E. G. & Heggie, J. F. (1972). Protective pathology laboratory coat. *Lancet*, i, 1271.

POST-MORTEMS ON PATIENTS WHO HAVE DIED OF VIRAL HEPATITIS TYPE B

ADVICE TO BE GIVEN TO UNDERTAKERS AND RELATIVES*

These patients have died of an infectious disease and the tissues and body fluids are still capable of transmitting infection. The body must be enclosed in a plastic bag.

Although the relatives may have risked infection from contact with the patient in life, it is reasonable to keep as small as possible any further risk of infection to relatives and to attendants dealing with the body.

The following recommendations are made:

1 The body should not normally be removed from the plastic bag except when a post-mortem examination is to be carried out.

2 After post-mortem examination the body should be put back in the plastic bag.

3 Viewing of the face, without physical contact, should be permitted and the body resealed in the plastic bag.

4 Further exposure of the body elsewhere will involve the further risk of releasing infectious material and should be avoided.

5 The embalming process reduces but cannot be guaranteed to eliminate the risk of infection from the body; it involves extraction of infected material from the body as well as further exposure of infected tissues. Embalming is therefore undesirable except in unusual circumstances.

6 If relatives ask to see the body they should be told that there is a risk of infection and that in their own interests it is better for them not to do so.

7 If the relatives insist on seeing the body they will be allowed to see the face but must be strongly discouraged from touching or kissing it.

8 If relatives ask if the patient died from an infectious disease they should be told that he did. Some relatives may also need to be told that reasonable precautions will be taken to

*Reproduced by kind permission of King's College Hospital.

ensure that further risks of spreading the disease are reduced to a minimum. Relatives who are worried about having already been exposed to infection may be referred to the Consultant Physician.

OPENING OF AMPOULES*

(Containing dried cultures issued by the National Collection of Type Cultures)

Identify the culture by the number on the paper inside the ampoule, reading from the round end of the tube.

The vacuum of each ampoule is checked before dispatch and should be confirmed if a high-frequency vacuum tester is available.

Care should be taken in opening the ampoule as the contents are in a vacuum. Make a file mark on the ampoule near the middle of the cotton wool plug and apply a red-hot glass rod to crack the glass. Allow time for air, filtered by the plug, to seep into the ampoule and then gently remove the pointed top part. Otherwise if the pointed part is snapped off the plug will be drawn to one end and hasty opening may release fine particles of dried organisms into the air of the laboratory. The plug may be impregnated with dried culture, and should be regarded as dangerous to handle and removed with forceps. Flame the open end of the tube and insert a sterile cotton wool plug (e.g. the plug from a Pasteur pipette). The discarded plug and the pointed end of the ampoule should be treated as infected and autoclaved.

About 0·5 ml of broth, when necessary enriched with blood, should be added to the ampoule and the contents carefully mixed so as to avoid frothing. Most of the organisms will be on the number paper. According to the gaseous and growth requirements, the broth suspension should be subcultured on to a suitable medium or media preferably chosen to include a solid medium, both to obtain single colonies and to detect aerial contaminants which may be introduced during the opening of the ampoule. The paper should be lifted out of the ampoule on a wire loop, the end of a Pasteur pipette or with forceps and placed on the surface of the solid medium with the number upwards. Ready recognition of the culture is thus ensured and confusion prevented if a number of cultures are opened. It is a wise precaution also to inoculate one or more additional media with the culture in the ampoule, as a precaution against any accidental difficulty.

---

*Reproduced by kind permission of the National Collection of Type Cultures (PHLS).

(EXTRACT FROM PHLS MONOGRAPH NO 6. THE PREVENTION OF LABORATORY ACQUIRED INFECTION. 1974 REVISED 1977) LONDON : HMSO

SITING OF SAFETY CABINETS AND ROOM VENTILATION

The cabinet must be at such a height from the floor that the operator looks through the glass front. Short operators may tend to work near to the sill and look under the glass shield. They should be provided with high seats and foot rests.

The length of trunking between cabinets and exhaust system should be as short as possible. Trunking and exhaust systems are described below. The cabinet must be placed away from doors and openable windows which may cause draughts (detectable by smoke tests) and in such a position that no-one walks in front of it, or behind the operator when it is in use. Cross currents and disturbances of this kind may cause turbulence which may overcome the pull of exhaust system (Chatigny and Clinger, 1969). The effect of walking in front of the working face is described by Steere (1971) in his chapter on Ventilation. A person walking at 3·2 km/hr (2 miles/hr) causes a disturbance of the order of 0·8 m/sec (176 feet/min) and this would bring back into the room any particles eddying in the front of the cabinet.

In Fig. 1 two satisfactory and two unsatisfactory sites are shown. Good working conditions are not secured by putting an exhaust protective cabinet in a small room, e.g. of less than 30m³ unless the volume of air in the room and the air supply to it are such that the exhaust system can operate efficiently.

In any room containing an exhaust protective cabinet there should be not less than 6 changes of air per hour (Department of Health and Social Security, 1970).

It may be necessary to provide additional ventilation, e.g. from louvres in the door or in an internal wall. Fire regulations must be observed when considering this. Direct ventilation from the external air should be avoided; in cold weather it will be unacceptable to the occupants and if it is not at room temperature it may not enter the cabinet but seep across the working face and create eddies into the room from the cabinet.

If the air in a room is normally removed by a plenum system problems may arise because of competition between this and the exhaust

Fig. 1. Siting of Cabinets in a room.

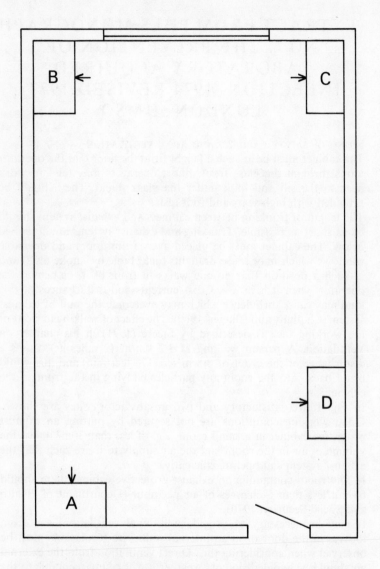

A & B are good sites, away from draughts between window and door and from pedestrian traffic.

C is not a good site, its performance may be affected by draughts between window and door.

D is a bad site in line with both draughts and pedestrian traffic.

system of the cabinet. They may interfere with one another or jointly remove too much air from the room, causing turbulence and reducing the efficiency of the cabinet exhaust. It is desirable that the room exhaust ducts be closed when the cabinet is being used. However, this may cause imbalance in the plenum system and disturb the ventilation of other rooms. The ventilation engineer should be consulted early in the planning of the room.

Where there is full air-conditioning, and warm air is ducted into a room there may be concern that it is promptly removed by the cabinet exhaust. This is unfortunate but irremediable. Safety must take precedence over cost.

In US laboratories, where air-conditioning is more popular than it is in the UK, they have overcome this difficulty (US Department of Health, 1976). When the cabinet exhaust leads into the ducts of a 'total loss' system it does so through a thimble unit which ensures that air is removed from the room either through the cabinet or through the normal outlet but not through both at the same time; this maintains the room air balance. A disconnect relay system is attached to the fan motor and the building air-conditioning system and provides automatic cut-off of the cabinet motor if the building system fails.

EXHAUST SYSTEMS AND THEIR SITING

A correctly designed centrifugal fan powered by an adequate electric motor is the only satisfactory exhaust system. A bunsen, burning just below the outlet, is quite useless.

The extract fan must be capable of giving a satisfactory face velocity at the working aperture and overcome both the resistance in the trunking and that caused by partial blocking by the filters.

With 6 m or less of 10 cm diameter smooth bore trunking with few bends, a fan which passes 0.1 m^3/sec, having a rotor of not less than 15 cm diameter and 5.6 cm width, rotating at 3000 rev/min should be satisfactory.

The fan unit must be mounted at the distal end of the trunking and discharge into the open air. This gives a negative pressure in the trunking and all leaks will be inward instead of discharging into the room.

Ideally the exhaust system should be mounted on the roof and the laboratory it serves be on the top floor of the building. If this is not possible the system may be mounted in a wall or in a window.

The aspect is important. If the fan outlet faces the prevailing wind efficiency will be reduced and it will be necessary to screen the aperture with a mushroom baffle or to trunk the effluent above the roof level. Problems may arise if the outlet is in the lee of the building or on the roof. When the prevailing wind is blowing against the building a 'cavity' may be formed (Steere, 1971). If the effluent is discharged into this cavity it may not be dispersed and diluted but may eddy into windows on the cavity of the building. Ideally the effluent should be carried above the cavity side by external ducting. This is very important if toxic vapours are generated in the cabinet but less important for adequately filtered microbiological effluents. Correct siting may be difficult to achieve when fitting exhaust systems to existing buildings and may lead to conflict with the planning authority. Advice should be sought from ventilation engineers.

The effluent should never be discharged near to the open windows of hospital wards.

An anti blow-back device should be fitted into the system to prevent infected material being dislodged from the filter and returned to the cabinet or the room when there are exceptionally high winds. Wire meshing across the aperture will prevent nesting by birds.

All outlets should be labelled to warn maintenance staff against obstructing them.

Some exhaust systems are very noisy. Vibrations from the motor may be transmitted to the cabinet via the trunking or to other parts of the room via the fabric of the building. The motor should be mounted on rubber pads and the trunking should not be fitted rigidly into the fabric. Exhaust units on the roof are usually less troublesome in this respect than those fitted into windows or walls. Noise from the latter may be reduced by enclosing the motor and fan in a box of expanded polystyrene which is ventilated only to the open air.

Excessive noise and vibration usually indicate a fault in the motor or an imbalance of the fan.

TRUNKING

The trunking connecting the cabinet with the exhaust system should be as short as possible, and of smooth bore and should have the minimum of bends. It should be circular, not rectangular, in cross section. Curves rather than right angles should be used for bends; the radius of the curve should be not less than 2·5 times the diameter of the trunking. These factors reduce turbulence and drag. Plastic soil and drain piping, 10 cm or 15 cm diameter is suitable. A number of fittings and bends are available from builders' merchants. These fit together with internal sealing rings making assembly and maintenance easy. For large-radius bends, difficult offset bends and short straight runs, flexible trunking of aluminium foil and bituminous paper may be used, but the corrugated nature of this impedes air flow and the internal paper lining may become detached and partially block the lumen. It should therefore be used for

Fig. 2. Trunking systems.

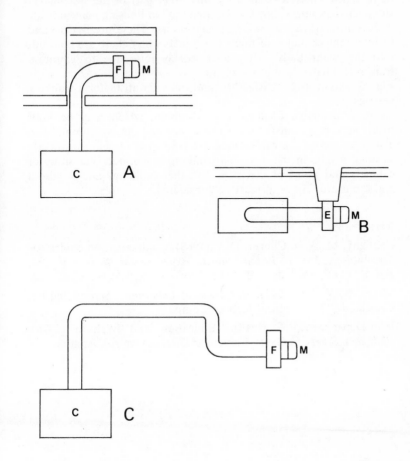

A shows elevation of cabinet exhausted through roof into a louvred roof cage. The trunking is short and there is one "easy" 90° bend, of flexible tubing to the fan unit.

B shows a similar arrangement in plan but exhausted through wall or window. The trunking could be offset by a $172\frac{1}{2}$° plastic soil pipe bend.

C shows a very unsatisfactory system. The trunking is too long, there are too many bends and these are too abrupt.

C – cabinet
F – fan
M – motor

short runs only and regularly inspected. The corrugations should be flattened where it connects to any other part of the system.

Connections to the cabinet spigot and the fan housing may be made with rubber sleeves or WC-pan connectors. These are flexible and facilitate the changing of filters in cabinets where these are not built into the main body. They also reduce noise due to vibration transmitted from the motor and fan.

Fig. 2 shows two satisfactory and one unsatisfactory trunking systems.

There is available commercially a cabinet which may be built firmly against an outside wall. The motor and fan are contained in a unit on top of the cabinet and the effluent is discharged directly through a hole in the wall. No trunking is required, but siting of cabinets and point of discharge to other buildings and windows and the prevailing wind must be considered.

REFERENCES

Chatigny, M. A. & Clinger, D. I. (1969). Contamination control in aero-biology. In: *An Introduction to Experimental Biology*, p. 194. *Eds*. R. L. Dimmick & A. B. Ackers. New York: Wiley-Interscience.

Steere, N. V. *Ed*. (1971). *Handbook of Laboratory Safety*, 2nd ed. Cleveland: The Chemical Rubber Company.

US Department of Health, Education and Welfare (1976). *Biological Safety Cabinets*. Center for Disease Control, Atlanta.

SELECTED REFERENCES

British Society for Clinical Cytology (1976). *Recommendations of a Working Party on Safety in Cytology Laboratories.*

Central Health Services Council (1968). Report of the Joint Committee on the *Care of the Health of Hospital Staff.* London: HMSO.

Chatigny, M. A. (1961). Protection against infection in the Microbiological Laboratory: Devices and Procedures. In: *Advances in Applied Microbiology.* Vol. 3, p. 131. *Ed.* W. W. Umbreit. London: Academic Press.

Collins, C. H., Hartley, E. G. and Pilsworth, R. (1977). *The Prevention of Laboratory Acquired Infection* (Public Health Laboratory Service Monograph No. 6). London: HMSO.

Collins, C. H. (1976/78). *Safety in Pathology Laboratories: a Bibliography.* Revised Edition. London: Institute of Medical Laboratory Sciences.

Department of Health and Social Security (1972). *Immunization Against Infectious Disease.* London.

Department of Health and Social Security *et al.* (1972). *Safety in Pathology Laboratories.* London.

Department of Health and Social Security *et al.* (1972). *Safety in the Post-Mortem Room.* London.

Department of Health and Social Security (1975). *Memorandum on the Control of Outbreaks of Smallpox.* London: HMSO.

Department of Health and Social Security *et al.* (1975). *Report of the Working Party on the Laboratory Use of Dangerous Pathogens.* (Chairman: Sir George Godber.) Cmnd. 6054. London: HMSO.

Department of Health and Social Security *et al.* (1976). *Control of Laboratory Use of Pathogens very Dangerous to Humans.* London.

Department of Health and Social Security *et al.* (1976). *Second Report of the Advisory Group on Testing for the Presence of Hepatitis B Surface Antigen and Its Antibody.* (Chairman: Sir William Maycock.) London.

Dowsett, E. G. and Heggie, J. F. (1972). *Protective Pathology Laboratory Coat. Lancet*, i, 1271.

Gajdusek, D. C. *et al.* (1977). Precautions in medical care of, and in handling materials from, patients with transmissible virus dementia (Creutzfeldt-Jakob Disease). *New England Journal of Medicine.* Vol. 297, No. 23. 1253.

Kelsey, J. C. and Maurer, I. M. (1972). *The Use of Chemical Disinfectants in Hospitals* (Public Health Laboratory Service Monograph No. 2). London: HMSO.

Maurer, I. M. (1972). The Management of Laboratory Discard Jars. In: *Safety in Microbiology*, p. 53. *Eds*. D. A. Shapton and R. G. Board (Society for Applied Bacteriology Technical Series No. 6). London: Academic Press.

Medical Research Council (1969). *Report by a Working Party on Pressure Steam Sterilizers. Lancet*, i, 424.

Percy-Robb, J. W., Proffit, J. and Whitby, L. J. (1970). Precautions adopted in a clinical chemistry laboratory as a result of an outbreak of serum hepatitis affecting hospital staff. *Journal of Clinical Pathology*, 23, 751.

Pike, R. M. (1976). Laboratory associated infections: Summary and analysis of 3921 cases. *Health Laboratory Science*, 13, 105.

Stern, E. L. and others (1974). Aerosol production associated with clinical laboratory procedures. *American Journal of Clinical Pathology*, 62, 591.

INDEX

	Page
Accident records	9
Accommodation, blood sampling	14
Category B work	13
for clothing	12
post-mortem room	37
rest room	12
reception	14
Air freight	18
mail (overseas post)	18
Ampoules	26
Animal pathogens from abroad	19
Anthrax	42
Autoclaves	21
Automated equipment	31, 34

Biohazard signs	13, 52
Biological safety cabinets	27 *et seq*
Blood sampling	14
Breakage and spillage	7, 26, 54
Broken and leaking specimens	7, 54
Browne's tubes	22

Catalase tests	34
Category A pathogens	1, 43
B1 pathogens	2, 3, 4, 10, 13, 14, 23, 24, 32, 33, 35, 36, 40
B2	3, 4, 10, 13, 14, 23, 24, 32 35, 36, 40
B1 accommodation	13
see also 'Danger of Infection', specimens	
C pathogens	4, 23
Centrifuges, infectious hazards	23 *et seq*
Chemical pathology, infectious hazards	31 *et seq*
Classification of pathogens	1 *et seq*
Clothing, accommodation	12
protective	10, 15, 37, 39, 43, 59
Containers, autoclaving	20
broken glass	21
incinerating	22
infected waste	20
'sharps'	20
specimen	16
Cosmetics	11
Cryostats	36, 56
Cytology, infectious hazards	36

71

		Page
'Danger of Infection' and High Risk		
specimens		3, 14, 15, 32, 33, 35
'Danger of Infection', warning signs		13, 52
Dangerous Pathogens Advisory Group		1
Dialyzer membranes		31
Discard containers, disinfectant		21, 23
Discarding specimens and cultures		20, 31, 33, 34
Disinfectants, laboratory		23, 55
post-mortem room		38, 55
testing with *Salm. typhi*		34
Distribution of infected material		16
Effluents, automated equipment		31, 32
Electron microscopy, infectious hazards		35
Exhaust protective cabinets		
disinfection and testing		27 *et seq*
Eye protection *see* Vizors		28, 57
Faeces, in chemical pathology		32
Food and drink		11, 37
Frozen sections		36
see also Cryostat		
Fume cupboards		57
Glass, broken		21
Griffith's tubes		25
Gloves, when worn		10, 15, 24, 26, 32, 35, 36, 37, 39
Haematology, infectious hazards		32 *et seq*
Hand basins		11
washing		11
Health of staff		7 *et seq*
Hepatitis B surface antigen ⎱		
virus ⎰		3, 9, 11, 13, 24, 32, 33, 35, 36, 41, 60
High Risk Specimens, *see* 'Danger of		
Infection', specimens		
Histopathology, infectious hazards		36
Homogenisers		25, 32
Immunisation		8, 32, 51
Incineration		22
Infectious hazards, chemical pathology		31
centrifuges		23 *et seq*
cytology		36

72

	Page
electron microscopy	35
histopathology	36
homogenisers	25
microbiology	34
post-mortem rooms	37 *et seq*
tissue culture	35
warning signs	13, 52
Infected material, distribution	16
treatment	19
Injuries	11, 37
Kampff microincinerator	29, 34
Labelling 'Danger of Infection', specimens	14
Laboratory infections, investigation	9
Laminar flow cabinets	27
Leaking specimens	7, 26, 54
Loops, bacteriological	34
Medical contact cards	8
fitness of staff	7
monitoring	9
records	9
Microbiology, infectious hazards	34
Microincinerators	29, 34
Needles, hypodermic	15, 19
Overseas air freight post	16, 18
Packing specimens and cultures	17 *et seq*
Personal precautions	9 *et seq*
Petri Dishes	34
Pipettes, disinfection	23
Pipetting	24
Plastic bags for specimens	14, 18
for discarded material	20
Posting pathological material	17
Post-mortem rooms, infectious hazards	37 *et seq*
Pregnancy	9
Preventive inoculations	8, 37, 51

	Page
Racks, specimen	14, 16
Reception and transport of specimens	14, 16, 47, 49
Records, health and accident	5, 9
References	69
Request forms, contaminated	26, 54
Rest rooms	12
Rubella	8
Safety Officer	5 *et seq*
of equipment	5
Salmonella infections, p-m room	40
Salmonella typhi, testing disinfectants with	34
Screening, staff health	8
Serum separation	15
Shakers and homogenisers	25
'Sharps'	20
Sickness	9
Sinks, disinfecting	31
Smallpox, precautions	43
Smoking	11, 37
Spattering, in bunsens	34
Specimen containers	16
reception and transport	14, 16, 47, 49
Spillage and leakage	7, 26, 54
Spore strips	22
Sputum	3, 13, 35
Sterilisation	21 *et seq*
Staff, domestic services	6, 45
clerical (office)	6, 48
clothing accommodation	12
engineering	7
graduate	6
health of	7 *et seq*
messengers	7, 49
model rules for	45, 47, 48, 49
office (clerical)	6, 48
porters	7, 49
reception	6, 47
technical	6
wash-up room (domestic)	6, 45
Syringes	20
Ten Broeck grinders	25
Test tape, autoclave	22
Thermocouples	21
Tissue culture, infectious hazards	35
grinders	25

	Page
Towels	11
Training staff	6
Tuberculosis	3, 8, 35, 41
skin tests and BCG	8, 37
Urines	23, 32
Vizors	15, 32, 39, 41
Viral hepatitis (*see* Hepatitis B)	
Washing facilities	11
Warning signs	13, 52
X-rays	7, 8, 37

Printed in England for Her Majesty's Stationery Office
by Oyez Press Limited, London

Dd 587160 K 284 6/78

Madigan shook his head slowly.

'This is sure some town for standing on its dignity,' he murmured only half-aloud, saw her face stiffen. 'He say anything about moving on?'

'I told you – he promised to come back the next day and we – we were to go for a drive out on the plains.'

Then he would have hired a surrey ... 'And he never showed and you never tried to get in touch?'

Her head moved haughtily. 'I just told you...!'

'Yeah, I know. You won't chase any man. But if you're asked to have supper with him by that snooty manager you jump to it, huh?'

She stood, rising to her toes, quite tall and looking quite dignified, if not offended by his remark.

'I believe your visit has just come to an end, Madigan... Please get out!' She flung an arm out towards the door and he stood up slowly, looking steadily at her until she lowered her eyes and her hands clasped uneasily in front of her gown.

'I've got a feeling I'll be back.' He touched a hand to the brim of his battered hat. '*Hasta luego, Señora Pascale.*'

Her face coloured and she stiffened,

mouth curling.

'Don't you throw that Mexican jargon at me, just because of my name! I'll have you know Mr Pascale was a gentleman rancher and one of the finest *hidalgos* who ever lived!'

Madigan smiled. 'You did all right, marrying an *hidalgo*. If you did he couldn't've left you too well off if you've got to resort to – companionship to make a living.'

'How dare you!' She strode towards him, her face turning ugly. 'You damn saddletramp, coming into my room with your trail smells and your ratty clothes and speaking to me like I'm some cheap whore...'

'No, ma'am. I never thought you were cheap.'

She went for his eyes and he caught her wrists. Then the door burst open and Sheriff Duane came in. He took in the situation swiftly, drew his sixgun and swung at Madigan's head. The marshal spun the large woman around and the gun barrel bounced off the upswept hairdo. She gave a strangled cry and fell to her knees, half-sobbing, half-moaning, holding both hands to her head. The sheriff was so surprised he stood there staring down at her, mouth hanging open, still holding the sixgun. He murmured a curse and started to bend down, then remembered Madigan and came spinning back.

Madigan's right hook took him on the side of the jaw and Duane crashed against the wall. He shook his head, dropping his gun, then charged back, eyes wild with fury.

Madigan blocked the first roundhouse swing, got under and took the second blow on his upper left arm. He winced as it hurt the old wound, then he rammed the top of his head into Duane's face. The man stumbled back, nose and mouth bleeding. Madigan closed, arms working, hammering the man in the body and, when Duane dropped his hands, pummelled his blood-streaked face. The sheriff's legs wobbled and he almost went down. Madigan put him down all the way with two short, punishing blows to the jaw.

Duane floundered, started to rise instinctively but without much co-ordination. Madigan kicked him in the head and he crashed back, out like a wind-blown match flame.

Madigan was pleased to note he wasn't breathing too heavily after his exertions. He reached down and helped the dazed woman to her feet. He pushed her across the room and let her fall across the bed. He stood over her as she moaned, tried to focus her eyes on him.

'What happened to Jay Sandlo?' he asked quietly, glancing towards Duane but the man would be out for a while yet.

She stared back uncomprehendingly. He asked again, grabbed a fistful of the kimono and shook her. The gown started to open and he rolled her on to her face, placed a knee between her shoulderblades, twisted his fingers in the topknot of her hair, pulling her head back. The motion brought a small cry from her and she writhed.

'Jay – Sandlo,' he gritted, pulling back harder.

She gagged and made choking noises, feebly trying to reach his wrists. He eased up the pressure.

She coughed. 'Damn – you!' He shook her impatiently, tightened his grip on her hair again. 'No! Don't – please!'

'I'm waiting but I won't wait long, *señora.*'
'All *right!*'

He allowed her to roll on to her back and she looked up at him, but the anger was mixed with pain and a thin trickle of blood oozed down her face.

'Don't mark my face. A man came to the

restaurant door, saw me with the senator and – and made a sign to me.'

'What kind of sign?'

She hesitated. 'To – take him upstairs to my room. I knew what he wanted me to do and he was already waiting when we got here...'

'And...?'

'He had two men with him. One of them – hit Jay from behind with a gun butt and they tied his hands and feet and...' She gestured to a window that led to a balcony. 'They took him out that way. That's all.'

'How much did they leave for you? *Come on!* It's obviously not the first time you've set up a man to be rolled for his money...'

'There was a hundred dollars under my pillow.'

'Now that's good pay... Normal?'

She hesitated. 'No. Usually it's – twenty-five... Look, my husband was a fool, gambled away the whole of his estate and–'

'Save it! I don't give a damn about you or your husband. I want to know who that man was who got you to bring Jay up here.'

'Just a man who comes to town occasionally and – we do business. I – I'm afraid to refuse him if you must know. He's a – terrifying man, extorts money from this place.'

'His name, goddammnit!' Madigan grabbed her hair again and she whipped her hands up to clasp his and take some of the pressure off her scalp.

'Wait! – You won't know him. He – he's local–'

'Jesus, lady, if you don't–'

She was afraid now and almost yelled:

'Daggett, a man named Mace Daggett!'

CHAPTER 7

STICK-UP!

The train coming in through the Wahoo Valley whistled as it approached the trestle-bridge above the river.

It was a mere formality because, although this was a single track, there was no possibility that it would meet another train coming from the opposite direction. The Wahoo Express, a dirty, rust-speckled freight, was the only train to use the line, bringing in hopper cars loaded with ore from the lead-mines between Osceola and the town of Wahoo.

It took supplies on the return run and occasionally the mine payroll. But most times this was carried by horse-drawn wagon with an armed escort that deterred most bandits. Those who tried their luck were either buried alongside the trail or serving time on the chain-gangs.

Now, as the train was on its way *in* to Omaha from the valley there was no reason to expect it would be carrying anything of value. Sure, the ore was worth many thousands but it had to be crushed and smelted and in any case there were hundreds of tons of it in the long snaking line of hoppers which writhed behind the big loco. A little more than any bandit could carry off in his saddle-bags. There was a paint-peeling caboose at the far end, not always manned. This run there were three miners hitching a ride into town for a few days leave and the train guard was glad of their company. But, being old, he was pretty much out of their rough-talk and what passed for conversation – comparing the charms or lack of them in various whores they aimed to see in Omaha.

So he dozed and left the others to their tall tales.

The engineer and stoker had done this monotonous run so many times that they could manage it in their sleep. Neither was very alert. The stoker prepared some slabs of buffalo steak to cook on the blade of the coal shovel thrust into the firebox, being liberal with the spices, for he thought the meat smelled as if it was going off. The engineer lounged in his seat after blowing the whistle, elbow on the iron window-ledge, hand cupped against the side of his head, swaying

96

in somnolent rhythm with the locomotive. Vaguely he heard the clacking as the wheels passed over the joints, the hiss of the pipes and the monotonous click of the big needle jumping on the main steam-pressure gauge. The stoker began to hum an Irish tune as he lifted the bar and swung the door of the fire-box open. The door clanged dully against the boiler and as he crouched, pushing the shovel blade with its spice-sprinkled, fat-glistening steaks into the flames, the engineer swore and jumped, leaping for the brake, winding the wheel frantically. The train lurched as the shoes clamped on the spinning wheels and the stoker screamed as he fell forward, out-thrust arm going into the fire and the bed of glowing coals. He fell, sprawling, the steaks sliding off the shovel to hiss and sizzle amongst the burning logs and coal.

'Christ, there's a buffalo on the bridge!' yelled the stunned engineer.

The stoker hugged his scorched shirt and burned arm to his chest but the engineer's words made him momentarily forget the pain – and his anger at the sudden stop. He blinked up at the engineer who was leaning far out of the cab now.

'Buffalo? They wouldn't walk out there – damn great clumsy animals! They'd break a leg on the ties...'

'This one din' walk,' the engineer said, ducking back into the cab, a tremor in his voice now. 'Musta been dragged. It's dead.'

'Who'd drag a dead buff... ?Judas! Injuns?'

'Dunno. I think I can see a rope around its neck and hind legs...'

'Rope don't sound like Injuns,' allowed the stoker, wincing as he peeled away the scorched cloth and saw his rapidly blistering arm. 'Oh, God! Look at my arm!'

But the engineer's attention was elsewhere. He watched with thudding and hammering heart as a group of bandanna-masked men came out of the bushes, all with guns ranging from double-barrelled Greeners through carbines to six-shooters. He stepped back, almost falling over the stoker as one rangy man jumped up on to the footplate, looked at both the railroad men with narrowed eyes, then braced himself against the grab-rail and cut loose with both barrels of his shotgun.

Down the train there were scattered shots as the miners and the sleepy-eyed train-guard traded lead with some of the bandits. One masked man stumbled and slid on the steep gravel slope. The miner who had shot him, in his excitement, leaned far out of the caboose and a train-robber with a red-and-white spotted bandanna masking the lower part of his face worked the lever and trigger of his carbine rapidly, the butt braced into his hip. Two bullets chewed splinters out of the caboose side and the other two slammed home into the miner's body. He jerked, lost his gun, tried to hold to the rail but missed his grip and tumbled out on to the slope. The wounded bandit, at the bottom of the slope now, reached up a beseeching hand.

'Help – me – Mace – I'm – belly-shot.'

'No use to me nor anyone else then,' Mace Daggett allowed above the gunfire and put a bullet through the man's head.

He turned back to the caboose, saw the old guard had fallen over the rail and lay sprawled on the tracks, unmoving. The other two miners called out they were out of ammo and tentatively showed themselves, hands held shoulder-high.

'C'mon out, if you're all through,' Daggett called. The men hesitated. *'C'mon!* Hell, we ain't gonna hurt you. You're no danger to us now.'

The two big men stepped down slowly, still looking worried. Daggett grinned behind his mask.

'Sit down on the track with your hands

clasped on top of your head,' he ordered. They obeyed. Daggett swung his eyes towards a rail-thin man who obviously had a large hawk nose, straining at the cloth of his bandanna mask. 'Billy, take care of these boys while we go collect our wages.'

The rail-thin man nodded, cradling his shotgun which he had reloaded after killing the train crew.

'You boys like a smoke?' he asked in a high, womanish voice. The miners glanced at each other, fighting to suppress grins at the sound coming out of this lanky ranny. 'No...? Well, OK, suit yourselves. Would be your last anyways!'

The shotgun jerked and thundered in two fast explosions. The miners were blasted half-way under the stationary wheels of the caboose.

By that time Mace Daggett and two more of his men had clambered up into the weathered old car. The two robbers set down their guns and began to move some crates and packages that were usually carried back here. They cleared the end wall, then the short, toadlike man took a crow-bar from his belt, rammed the chiselled end between the side wall and the end timbers of the panel, straining with a few grunts and many expletives.

The wall panel began to move out. He worked the bar in further and pried again. As the panel loosened more it began to tilt. The second man took the weight and together they swung it to one side. Daggett watched as they struggled with it awkwardly and leaned it against a side wall.

He thrust them out of the way and moved into the cavity now exposed. Only one small part was taken up although a man could have stood in there between the outside caboose wall and the fake panel just removed.

On the floor were two iron-bound boxes, each locked with two heavy padlocks. Daggett pulled down his red bandanna now, revealing a stubbled face with heavy lips drawn back in a triumphant grin.

'Just like the man said.' He jerked his head at the others, the wall panel now precariously propped up. 'Grab 'em and let's go. We'll open 'em back at camp.'

'What the hell's in there, Mace?' asked the toad-like man, panting as he and his companion lifted one box.

Daggett grinned. 'Maybe lead ain't the only thing they get outta that Wahoo mine, Jerry... C'mon. let's go!'

Beaumont T. Kimble figured he would give up on this chore come sundown unless he could find more fresh tracks by then. He had been mighty riled at himself for turning to drink again, just because of his mild fracas with the senator over his shooting the damn stag. The fight in the bar and with the whore had eased his tensions some but that pesky damn sheriff had riled him again by making him serve a couple of days in jail. After he had offered to pay for the damage done to the Wolf's Den too.

'Sure. You'll pay up, all right,' Duane had said with his usual unsmiling face. 'And you'll do extra time, too.'

'*Extra* time! How much?'

'For as long as I say!' Duane snapped. Kimble brooded in the cell, figuring he would break out if necessary.

But Duane was one of those men who simply had to have the last say about anything. *Insecure,* Beau reckoned. He had learnt that much from the strange Viennese doctor his father had insisted he see after he had gotten himself into a heap of trouble with guns, women and booze. Man had some crazy notions – called himself a doctor of the human mind...

That would be enough to make anyone

wary, having an appointment with someone with a title like that– Still, he had felt better after several visits, *expensive* visits, his father kept reminding him.

'Now I don't mind – long as it does some good,' Harlan Kimble had told him. 'I've got great hopes for you, son. I know you still have that damn childish dream of being a gun-toting marshal and I'll do a deal with you: you stop your boozing and trouble-making and I'll see what I can do about getting you into the Marshals Service.'

Beau had curled his lip at the bribe at first, but admitted to himself in private that he *would* still like to be a marshal. Well, why not? There wasn't much else that appealed to him, which was why he tried to find an outlet for his frustrations and energy in booze and fights. But first he had to try and shake that Virginian professional virgin who was clinging to him, her eye on his money – or his father's money, to be exact.

Well, there had been trouble, as expected, but he had still gotten into the Marshals Service, and for the first time he ran up against a little real criticism. He didn't count Madigan's harsh censure during training because the man had a knack of backing up his words and showing you how to manage what you'd previously made a mess of, but first time that the senator tore into him with harsh words, he had reacted like the spoilt brat he used to be, thrown his tantrum, poured booze down his throat.

OK! No more! That was a promise to himself. He had broken a lot of promises in his short life but this was one he aimed to keep.

Now Senator Jay Sandlo had disappeared without trace. He had panicked a little at first, sent off that wire, screaming for help, to Parminter. He felt like kicking his own tail till his nose started to bleed for going off half-cocked that way. He blamed the hang-over and his anger at Duane's treatment of him.

Beau knew he wouldn't win any points with Parminter, sending that telegram. If it had simply been a message informing him that the senator had run into some kind of trouble, that would have been fine. But to add on to that information: NEED HELP! STRANGE COUNTRY – NO CLUES. PLEASE SEND MAN WHO KNOWS THIS AREA. MAYBE BRONCO. URGENT.

He felt uneasy even now, traipsing through country that was going to beat him, he knew, if he didn't get a hold of himself.

Madigan – or someone – ought to be in Omaha now. So, if he couldn't find any hopeful tracks by sundown, he would head back there.

It wasn't that he was afraid of running into the men who had kidnapped Sandlo – he had gotten that much out of the woman who worked the Blue Star. It was just this feeling that he somehow didn't know what he was doing. He had found some signs, lost them, made his way to a couple of isolated ranches and learned at one that a group of riders had been seen passing to the south. The men on the other ranch were so obviously working on the very edge of the law that he took no notice of any 'information' they had given him.

Maybe I should've. Maybe they wanted to get back at some rivals and have that neck of the woods to themselves.

The more he thought of it, the more confident he felt that he could be right. Now what had those two shifty-eyed hardcases said?

'Ain't seen nothin' lately, but there's a place back there in Dark Canyon they say is used by some owlhoots. They'd be the ones you might be interested in.'

Sceptical, Kimble had been about to say

something when the second man spoke.

'Hard men in that bunch. Chip an' me, we stay clear of 'em. They ride the left fork and we keep to the right in our own bailiwick...'

There it was! In our own bailiwick!

The man was practically telling him that they were giving him gospel information. They saw him as a way of getting rid of the opposition; he was sure rustling and worse was widespread in this area.

The *left* fork...

He had actually followed their directions as far as Dark Canyon but had ridden down the right fork of the trail. As it had led nowhere – the hardcases' spread visible in the distance – he had figured they were just giving him the runaround, having fun with a greenhorn.

Dark Canyon was far over the range now. He could just about make it by sundown, camp above the left fork in the trail, make a sashay down it before sun-up, when tracks were easier to read.

Decision made now, Kimble climbed back into the saddle of his patient, though tiring horse, and set about finding his way out of this maze of hills and draws and dry gulches. He would never have believed this country was anything but flat as skillet – until he arrived here.

Now, all he had to do was find the senator – still alive.

He hesitated a little, slowing the horse as it started the climb out of the ravine, close to tumbling water that lifted a fine spray like a light fog to his left. Maybe he'd better wait for Madigan, or whoever Parminter had sent. Someone who knew the country.

'Hell, no!' he said aloud and felt such relief at this quick decision that he repeated it, with emphasis on the *hell!*

He had made enough of a fool of himself. Time to prove he had what it took to be a good marshal.

If he could bring Senator Jay Sandlo back alive and well – more or less – then his stock would rise mighty fast with Parminter. And Madigan.

He wondered why it seemed more important to have Madigan's approval than that of the chief marshal...?

There were enough things to wonder about already so he pushed that to the back of his mind and concentrated on the trail, glancing up at the sun, angled over steeply now.

It was going to be close.

He reached the area of Dark Canyon with

still an hour left before dark. There was a good camping-place on the slope, near a fresh-water spring, and it gave him a view of the actual trail before it forked, left leading into the canyon, right taking him back in a long sweeping arc to where he had spoken with those hardcases.

He made it a small camp, digging a trench for his fire, just big enough to warm-over a can of beans and some sowbelly he had been saving. He placed rocks around the trench and as soon as the food was warm enough threw dirt over the fire. He washed the meal down with canteen water fresh from the spring and admitted that the drink was the best thing about the meal. It was cold on the slopes and he had just got his heavy jacket out of his warbag, started levelling some ground to spread his bedroll when, in the half-light, he saw four or five horsemen – it was hard to make them out against the black granite of the hills over there – riding into the canyon. They were leading two pack-mules, took the left fork.

Kimble was mounted and riding away from the camp within minutes, keeping dark scrub at his back so he would be hard to see should one of the riders look this way. But no one had seen him by the time he reached the left fork and, heart racing a little, he heeled his mount forward.

The place was well named. The rocks and brush and overhanging trees made it like full night although back on the flats on the approach it was still light enough to read by. The trail was narrow so he didn't have to look for tracks and he followed warily, Mannlicher rifle in hand, sixgun loosened in his holster, his body tense in the saddle.

Beau Kimble wasn't sure how long it took him – a half-hour at most he later reckoned – but although he hadn't sighted the riders again he could still sniff the dust left by their passage hanging in the air. He could even smell the sweat of their mounts. Several times he paused, listening hard, but the evening insects and homing birds fouled his hearing so that he was unable to pick up any other sound.

There was only one way they could have gone after rounding a rock that almost blocked the trail. He had had to dismount and lead his frightened horse around the narrow ledge above a small ravine which, he found, opened out into a box canyon.

He saw a camp-fire in there, outside a cave or a lean-to built up against a canyon wall, the flickering light making it difficult to be sure. Kimble found a safe spot to ground-hitch his horse, made sure he had a fully loaded spare magazine for the Mannlicher rifle and then clambered across the slope on foot, going to ground amongst some boulders which overlooked the outlaws' camp.

When he had first seen the men from his own campsite he hadn't thought to look for the senator, for it seemed to him that all the riders were free in the saddle, not bound to the horn like a prisoner would be.

Now he strained to see down there where the men were dismounting rowdily. He could hear the shouts but was unable to make out the words clearly from where he was. Two men came out of the cave or lean-to or whatever it was, stopping beyond the firelight's glow. He could not make out anything familiar about them.

Then the big man down by the fire, the one with the spotted red neckerchief called clearly,

'Senator, get on down here.'

It was Senator Jay Sandlo, all right. Not bound in any way that Kimble could see, but escorted by a second man who had come out of the cave.

They stopped in front of the chests, looking down at them. The man in the red bandanna said something and the senator snapped his head up. There was a brief argument. It looked to Kimble as though the senator was resisting. The big man grabbed his arm and pointed to the chests. Kimble distinctly saw Senator Jay Sandlo shake his head. The man with the red neckerchief drew his sixgun quickly and rammed the muzzle against Jay's temple.

Kimble couldn't hear the hammer cock from this distance, but he knew it was thumbed back by the man in the red bandanna.

The threat was plain to see: *do something to those chests*, (open them most likely) – *or get your head blown off.*

Contents

List of Illustrations   vii
A Personal Note   ix

PART ONE
Queens and Heirs Apparent
1

PART TWO
Portrait of a Lesbian Affair
123

PART THREE
Chacun Sa Tour
225

Sources and Bibliography   309
Index   331

CHAPTER 8

DEADLY NIGHTSHADES

Beau Kimble felt like his belly was solid ice. He literally couldn't move for a few moments.

His heart was somersaulting in his chest. Leastways, that was the feeling he had, along with another uncomfortable sensation of a prickling of his skin as if all his nerve ends were being pulled through.

Slowly, the tension eased and he settled into a more comfortable position, pushing up his hat so the brim wouldn't cut off his view from what was happening down in the far end of the box canyon. The senator's life was clearly in danger and it was up to him do something about it. *Now!*

He was one man against six or seven, and while he could easily pick them off with the Mannlicher he knew that after the first shot the others would be under cover in an instant. Sooner or later *he* would end up being the one pinned down.

Not only that, they might shoot the senator on the spot. Still, if they needed him to open those chests, maybe not. But he couldn't take that chance.

The tall man was still arguing with Jay Sandlo. *Stall 'em a little longer, senator! Just a little longer....!*

He had to get closer and see and hear what was going on. And find out what was in those heavy chests.

Gathering his rifle to him, making sure the safety catch was 'on' as he had already used the bolt to bring a cartridge up into the breech, Beau slithered back and stood up when he was in the deep shadow. His horse made a small whinny and stamped its foot and he murmured, 'Quiet!', turning towards it at the same time.

A shape came hurtling out of the brush and slammed into him, a hand groping for his gun arm as he was carried back by the sheer weight of the charge. Beau tripped and went down, rolled quickly and let go the rifle. He kicked the man away from him, slid back on his shoulders and reached for his holstered sixgun.

The attacker wasn't expecting him to give up the long arm so readily and was left rising to his knees, holding the Mannlicher, blinking. But he soon swung it round. His finger found the trigger, but there was no give because of the safety catch.

It was probably the last thought he had as Beau, still rolling, came up on one knee, sixgun blazing instinctively. The man was smashed back by the slug at this close range and the rifle fell with a clatter. Beau swore. That was the last thing he should have done.

A gunshot in the night.

Well, that's done it now!

The gunshot echoed and slapped around the enclosing walls of the box canyon. He saw the men around the fire on their feet already scattering for cover. *Where the hell had the Senator gone...? He couldn't see him in that chaos.* Well, he had nothing to lose now. He snatched up the Mannlicher, thumbed off the safety stud and beaded a running man, hardly leading him at all at this range. The whipping snarl of the rifle slapped at his ears and the man was going down even as the empty cartridge case flew out of the port. The bolt worked and slammed home a fresh shot. Beau fired again and a man stumbled, rolled, half-rose, dragging one leg. In his hurry, Beau worked the bolt too fast, jammed the empty case halfway out of the port.

Then he was in trouble with lead flying

around him, men shouting. The man he had shot, badly wounded, was reaching for his gun and shooting wildly. Beau lunged forward and slammed him in the head with the butt of the useless rifle. It would take too long to clear the mangled cartridge case now.

He ran to his horse, whipping his head back and breaking his stride as a bullet fanned past his face. He stumbled against the horse. It took two stabs to get the rifle seated in its scabbard, but the animal was already moving while he had only one boot in the stirrup.

The men down at the camp were shouting louder than ever now. He threw his body awkwardly across the saddle as the mount took off. His legs tore through the brush, banged against a sapling and slewed him around. The saddle horn rammed painfully into his side and then, gasping for breath, he managed to get one leg across, He slid into the saddle properly. Just in time to see a low tree branch racing at him with the speed of an express train.

Frantically, he ducked – not quite fast enough. There was a smashing impact above his eyes and his hat went flying as he was almost unseated. Somehow he managed to grip the reins hard enough and short enough to avoid being thrown. Almost out to it, the world exploding in fireworks and clanging bells, he slumped forward, his now bloody face buried in the horse's whipping mane.

He had enough sense left to do two things: twist the reins around his wrist and to croak into the mount's laid-back ear to run – 'Run like – *hell!*'

Then there was body-wrenching jolting – and darkness.

A *lot* of darkness.

Madigan didn't know the Nightshades country all that well. He had worked up around Omaha before but it had been years ago and things had changed. He didn't know the land this far north although he had passed through on the railroad.

The Nightshade Mountains were a strange series of ragged hills, the rims of long-dead volcanoes. The soil was rich in minerals on the slopes on one side of these hills, but on the other side the lifeless topsoil could be measured in inches. This gave the hills a lopsided appearance; rich, green vegetation on the slopes with the deep red soil, the 'inside' of the crater-rims, parched-looking scrub and brush with stunted trees on the other. There were basalt and granite canyons in there, too, twisting and turning, ranging from shallow draws to deep, steep-sided canyons. The water was chancy – it could be fresh and exhilarating, or loaded with minerals that would pucker a man's lips for days at a time and shrivel his tongue to boot.

He wished he had thought to bring an Osceola guide with him.

Madigan rode a sorrel and led a speckled black as a packhorse. He had come prepared to spend as long as was necessary to locate Jay Sandlo. They had known each other during the War and had spent several furloughs whooping it up but had lost contact after Appomattox. They had met on a couple of occasions since, once with Madigan along as a bodyguard for the then-new senator. Jay had indulged his favourite pastime of hunting and the old rapport they had experienced as comrades in arms surfaced once again. Madigan hadn't really followed Sandlo's career but he picked up information here and there and knew the man was honest and no-nonsense, an oddity among politicians of the day.

If for no other reason than their association in the Missouri Loyals, Bronco Madigan aimed to get Sandlo safely out of Mace Daggett's hands.

When the woman, Fern Pascale, had told him about the abduction of the senator, he had been stunned for a spell. Then he had roughed her up a bit, not only to get more information out of her, but to make sure she was telling the truth and not making up some story just to earn herself sympathy or put her in a good light.

During the interrogation, Sheriff Duane had started to come round and Madigan had leaned down and knocked him unconscious again with his sixgun barrel.

'You'll kill him!' Fern Pascale wailed and there was a look in her eyes that made Madigan think maybe there was some deeper relationship between them than simply lawman and high-class whore.

It wouldn't be unusual, if the lawman was being paid to turn a blind eye to her activities at the Blue Star. Many a corrupt lawman took some of his pay-off in kind.

'Just don't want him interfering,' Madigan told her, seeing more blood oozing from the deep cut on Duane's forehead as he turned back to the woman. 'If you've dealt with Mace Daggett and his snakes before, you must know where he hangs out.'

She was shaking her head before he had finished speaking.

'No! I swear! He – he shows up sometimes downstairs when I'm with a – male companion and if he makes his signal, I take the man up to my room. Usually – usually he just holds the man up for his money and threatens him so he'll stay quiet. Many are married men so – they obey.'

'Besides which, Daggett can be a frightening kinda *hombre* to have threatening you.'

This time she nodded emphatically. 'Yes!' she said in a low, almost hushed voice. 'He can be very – frightening.'

Madigan showed no sign of sympathy.

'So can I when I set my mind to it. You must have some idea where Daggett hangs out if this is a more or less regular thing.'

'No! Oh, no – he just – appears and–'

He grabbed her wrist and twisted, making her gasp as she sprawled on the bed again.

'Lady – and I use the term loosely – I don't have time to *talk* you around. You're in the cheap badger game no matter how you want to dress it up. In other words, you're breaking the law and you can go to jail for it. Or – I'm in a hurry, and I can mark you up some so that you'd have one helluva time getting any male 'companion' to even look at you – let alone want to share a meal or a bed with you. If you were scared of what

120

Daggett might do to you, take my advice – be a lot more scared of what I might do. A helluva lot more scared.'

She was pale and shaking, her eyes bulging. The thin layer of outraged sophistication had dropped away minutes earlier. Fear had taken over.

'Who are you?' she hissed, cringing.

'I'm the man asking you for the last time: where do Mace Daggett and his snakes hole up? I don't have a watch, but I'll count out ten seconds. After that...'

He reached down and unstrapped one of his spurs and held it in front of her terrified face. He thought for a moment she was going to faint.

He just managed to catch the words she croaked:

'Somewhere in – the Nightshades...'

That was about all she knew. He was convinced of that but she made one last lunge at him as he put his spur back on, trying for his eyes. He slugged her and it caught her on the side of the jaw. She collapsed across the bed. He left her there, locked the door after him, made haste to the livery where he hired his horses, learned that Beau Kimble had rented a dun and had mentioned he was going hunting in the Nightshades.

He would have liked to have had a word with the whore Beau had been with but there was no time. The senator was in real danger, in the hands of a murderous son of a bitch like Mace Daggett. Might already be dead.

If he was, Daggett and his men would soon join him, Madigan swore to himself – and it was no idle threat.

Night fell early in the Nightshades. He figured to camp out and venture in come sun-up. If Daggett was hiding out in there he would have night guards posted for sure. Daytime, too, but Madigan reckoned he would have a better chance of spotting and handling them than in the dark.

He found a small creek, tasted it and found it had a mild mineral bite that was palatable. He looked around. A few yards away, there were some boulders where he could spread his bedroll and make a camp-fire where it couldn't be seen. He was on a side of the hills where the soil was poor and there was only scrub and stunted trees for cover. The rocks suited him fine.

He dismounted and began to loosen the sorrel's cinch, looking across its back at the Nightshades and noting how dark it was in those folds of hills. Then he stopped all movement, swore softly as the horse snorted. He thought he had heard gunfire. Distant – in fact a long way off, just the dying echoes in those dark shadows.

He waited but didn't hear any more, decided he was mistaken, and continued with his chores and the setting-up of his camp. On a deal like this, he didn't cook anything, just heated water in the battered tin pot to make some coffee. The sizzling of meat frying in a skillet could easily mask the approach of an enemy, four-legged or two. So he ate beans out of a can, munched some cold biscuits that were on the point of being too stale to swallow. The coffee had an odd taste because of the mild minerality of the water but it warmed him as the cold winds of night blew down out of the Nightshades.

He ground-hitched both horses, spread his bedroll in a narrow space between two low rocks and levered a shell into his rifle's breech, afterwards lowering the hammer for safety. He took the rifle under the blankets with him, hunched down, tugging his hat over his eyes. Man, it felt good to stretch out and unkink stiff muscles. He hadn't slept for almost forty hours but sleep didn't come immediately.

There were night sounds, but strange ones

to him in these hills. The scream of a night-bird had his hand tightening swiftly around the rifle. It could be the cover for an Indian signalling to others moving in silently on his camp. Down in Texas, or in Montana or Wyoming, and likely a dozen other places, he would have been out of his blankets by now, sprawled between the rocks, gun hammer cocked, eyes straining into the darkness. Here, because of the cold and the strangeness of the place, he snugged under and cursed the bird for disturbing his rest. Indians weren't much of a problem in this neck of the woods.

And it *had* been a genuine call of a night-bird, but if he had been just a little more alert, less weary and cold, he might – just might – have heard the muted snap of a twig, the slow crunch of dry leaves under a boot as a man moved in on the rockpile where he sheltered.

The first he knew of it was when a foot thudded into him and skewed him out of his bedroll and a shotgun barrel rammed against his ribs.

A voice from the top of the dark shadow that towered above him snarled,

'Just move slow and easy, you son of a bitch, or I'll blow the top of your head off!'

CHAPTER 9

OUTLAWS

While Madigan collected himself, getting his breath back slowly, the intruder moved to the fire's coal bed and kicked some tinder in. As it flared, he also toed in some kindling and a small fire blazed.

Madigan groaned as he recognized Sheriff Duane. The man had a bandage around his head and his face looked haggard, his mouth mean. The shotgun barrels followed Madigan's every move.

'Shuck the Colt,' Duane ordered with a jerk of the Greener. 'Easy does it or I'll blow you in two right now.'

'What're you waiting for?' Madigan asked, genuinely curious. The lawman was plenty mad, that was plain to see, and his head must be throbbing like an Indian drum at a rain-dance. He had Madigan cold-decked. All he had to do was pull the triggers.

'I want to know just who the hell you are. You ain't the drifter you let folk think.'

Madigan eased his sixgun from the holster, using thumb and forefinger, held it out to his side and let it fall not far from his bedroll. Duane smiled crookedly, stepped across and kicked the gun out of reach, beyond the small spread of firelight. *Maybe he could shake up the sheriff* Madigan thought, and said,

'I'm a US marshal, Duane. Here to find Senator Jay Sandlo.'

It surprised the sheriff, all right, and his jaw dropped some.

'Well, you never even had the courtesy to tell me! But you could be. I've heard of a hardcase marshal named Madigan. Kill a man quick as look at him.'

'Only if I'm sure he's broken the law. You're riding the edge right now, Duane. I'm not quite sure if you're in something with Daggett or not.'

That startled the sheriff even more and he stepped back a pace, licked his lips and shifted his grip on the Greener. He was standing on the corner of the bedroll; Madigan was still sitting beside it, one hand gripping the askew blankets. He gave a mighty heave, rolling backwards, up on to his shoulders, then completing the backward somersault as the shotgun thundered and tore the night apart.

Duane didn't go down, but he staggered wildly. The Greener fired the second barrel as he tried to bring the weapon around to bear on the moving marshal. Dust and grit sprayed from the raking charge of buckshot and Madigan threw one hand in front of his face, stinging from the gravel. He dug in his boots and lunged forward as Duane got his balance and started to lift the shotgun so as to swing it at the marshal's head.

Bronco ducked under and drove a fist into Duane's belly. The man's breath *whooshed* and he staggered, doubled over. Madigan straightened, wrenched the empty shotgun free and used his body-weight to knock Duane to his knees. The sheriff threw himself at the hand that held the Greener, his sheer weight tearing it out of Madigan's grip. But the sheriff didn't get a chance to use the weapon as a club. Madigan kicked him in the chest and when he fell, stomped on the forearm above the hand gripping the Greener. The gun fell free and Duane flung a handful of gravel into Madigan's face, following it up with a roaring grunt, both arms swinging. The marshal ducked but not fast enough. Two blows cannoned off his head, turning him awkwardly. The attack moved to his body, fists hammering at his ribs, boots kicking at his legs.

Madigan stumbled, caught a boot as the next kick swung higher, twisted savagely with teeth bared, and heaved Duane across the campsite. The man went into one of the boulders and groaned, one leg buckling as the breath was beaten from him. Bronco came in with fists hammering a brutal tattoo, first on the man's upper body, then his face, one blow landing on the bandage on Duane's head. The cloth cushioned the force a little and saved Madigan a broken hand, but Duane wavered and lurched forward, hands reaching out towards Madigan for support.

The marshal slapped them aside, grabbed Duane's shirt and spun him around, slamming him back against the boulder. The sheriff gagged, his legs turned to wet paper and he started to fall. But Madigan kept hold of the front of his shirt, bared his teeth with the effort of holding the sheriff half-upright. With his free hand, which was throbbing from hitting Duane's head, Madigan batted the dazed man back and forth across the face. Duane struggled feebly, his eyes wide and angry at first, but as Madigan shook him, ramming him back against the rough rock time and again, and the big, calloused hands beat his cheeks and nose to pulp, he slowed and sagged, blood splashing on to the front of the marshal's jacket.

Panting, Madigan let him fall as far as his knees, then used a leg to pin the barely conscious man in that position. He pushed his head back until it hit the rock and the blood-streaked face was upturned, dim firelight glinting from the thin red rivers crawling across the bruised flesh.

'You in some deal with Daggett?'

Duane's swollen eyes were dulled with pain and he looked blankly at the marshal. Madigan shook him again, the man's head rapping painfully on the boulder.

'Jesus! Don't!'

'Answer me. Or I'll turn your head to mush!'

Duane's head bobbed loosely and it took Madigan a moment to realize the sheriff was nodding.

'Yeah! – Yeah! We – worked that – badger game – with Fern...'

'But it was different with the senator.'

Duane hesitated, then nodded.

'Daggett's idea, I think. Mighta been – Fern's. Hold him for – ransom.'

'You'd have to be plumb loco to try that!'

'What I told – Mace. But he – he said we could get – thousands, Sandlo bein' a –

senator.' He paused and Madigan was about to speak, realized Duane was thinking about something and waited. 'I – had me a notion – that Mace was holdin' out on me. I – I think he wanted the senator for – somethin' else – but he wasn't tellin' me what...'

Madigan frowned. 'What could he want him for?'

'I – dunno. Just a few things he said...'

He made gulping sounds and Madigan wheeled aside as the man threw up and fell sprawling, hands reaching out to stop himself sliding down the slope.

A rifle crashed out of the darkness.

Duane jerked at the same time as Madigan heard the smack of the bullet striking flesh, then the rifle fired again and Duane, already spinning, jumped as the second shot struck home. He fell, unmoving, shirt stained with fresh blood.

Madigan was already diving into the shadows where he knew his sixgun was, and his hand was closing over the butt when someone called,

'You OK, Bronco?'

He froze, recognizing the voice of Senator Jay Sandlo. Lying half on his back, cocked Colt in his hand, Madigan answered and started to clamber to his feet.

'Yeah, I'm all right, Jay...'

'Thank God for that! I had my rifle ready as I made my way towards your camp, and then saw him going for you.' The senator appeared in the dim light, glancing briefly at Duane, smiling at Madigan. 'When I heard that shotgun go off – twice – I figured someone had just found out if there is a life after death. Good to see you, Bronco!'

He lowered the rifle in one hand and thrust out his right towards the marshal. Madigan took it and was pulled easily to his feet. They stood only inches from each other and shook hands.

'You, too, Jay. But too bad you shot Duane.'

'Is that who it was? Well, what d'you mean, too bad? He was making a try for you, wasn't he? I saw him.'

'We'd had a bit of a go-round and I was just getting him to talk when he threw up. That's what all the ducking and weaving was about...'

'Aw, shoot! I thought he was trying to kill you! Sorry, Bronco. Maybe he's still alive? No. I guess not. I nailed him twice and that second shot was aimed at his ticker.' The senator nudged Duane's still form. There was no sign of life. 'Tell you what you wanted to know?' When Madigan didn't answer, he thumbed back his hat. 'What're you doing up here, anyway, Bronco? Thought Miles wouldn't let you do fieldwork.'

'Made him see reason. Anyway, Beau Kimble sent a wire that you'd disappeared. Asked for help.'

'Good old Beau. Yes. I was stupid. Fell for a woman's wiles, walked right into Mace Daggett in her room.'

Madigan nodded, studying the senator.

'Talked with Fern. Was getting some more information out of Duane when you walked in – out of nowhere.' There was a question in Madigan's last words and the senator looked uncomfortable.

'I guess it's going to be some time before I live this one down. Look, Bronco, they slugged me as soon as I followed Fern into her room and when I came to I was tied to my saddle. I passed out again and next time I surfaced, I was a prisoner in Daggett's camp.' He gestured. 'Back there somewhere in these hills.'

'You don't remember where?'

'No-ooo. You see, what happened, they went off somewhere, Daggett and most of his men. I figure it might've been to pull a job. When they came back, they were wild and whooping like a bunch of Apaches. Then next thing someone starts shooting into the camp and they scattered and grabbed their guns. Whoever it was did the shooting took off and Daggett yelled 'Looks like that damn kid who rode in with Sandlo!' – and they hit the saddles and went after him.'

Madigan frowned.

'*All* of them? They left you alone in the camp?'

Sandlo shook his head quickly.

'No, feller called Splinter stayed to watch I didn't get away. But he was anxious for the others to return and didn't watch me as closely as he should have. I managed to saw through my bonds, hit him with a rock, grabbed my guns and horse and tried to find my way out of these damn hills. The sound of the shotgun brought me down here.' He grinned and shrugged. 'Guess I was pretty lucky, huh?'

'Yeah. You OK? No after-effects?'

The senator looked a little blank, then lifted his hat and gingerly rubbed at the back of his head.

'Just a goose-egg bump and a headache I don't believe I've ever matched, not even after a night on the town with you.'

Madigan smiled. 'And there's been a few.'

'Say! You remember that wingding we

threw in Cross Keys after we beat those Yankees at the river ferry? Now the headache I had after *that* comes close to what I'm suffering right now, or maybe that other time at–'

'Jay! If that was Beau shooting up Daggett's camp and they went after him we'd better start looking, too.'

The senator's face became abruptly sober. 'Of course! I'm a bit shook-up. Not thinking straight yet, Bronco.' He gave a quick on-off smile. 'Been out of the action side of things for too long – not like you, come up against this kind of thing almost every day.'

'Not quite, but a lot more regularly than you, I guess. Yeah, I understand, Jay. But let's get going. You got any idea at all of the direction?'

Senator Jay Sandlo looked all around and shrugged, spreading his arms.

'Take your pick. I don't know where the hell I am in these hills, or which way I took to get here.'

Just then there came a faint, distant rattle of gunfire. They both jerked their heads around and looked out over the black hills and the clearly burning stars.

Madigan pointed towards Polaris.

'That way,' he said and sprinted for his horse.

Beaumont T. Kimble knew he had been spotted even before they started shooting.

His head was throbbing and his ears roaring and his eyes kept going in and out of focus. He was queasy, too, and had thrown up once. There was a large swelling across his forehead and blood had trickled into his left eye, making the lid sticky and adding even more difficulty to seeing properly. He felt terrible and would have given just about anything to be able to crawl into a bunk somewhere and fall asleep.

He gave his dun its head mostly, but once in a while jerked the reins a little just to let it know he was still in the saddle and still the boss. But he wasn't thinking clearly and there were short periods when he forgot what he was doing – either that, or he didn't seem to care, his brain not registering the trouble he was in. By the time it got through to him that he was now riding back *down* the slope instead of keeping to the high trails, it was too late.

There on the slope below were a couple of riders and they had their heads tilted, looking up-slope towards him. The hill was mostly bare on this side and he knew he would be silhouetted against the stars. His vision had cleared, at least temporarily, but it did nothing to make him feel any better.

Beau was still wheeling the dun up-trail when the rifles began their death-song, the shots crackling and echoing through the canyons and hills of the Nightshades. Naturally, it would alert the others who were hunting him, too. Even as the thought burned into his aching brain, he heard a shout ahead and another, a little fainter, slightly above.

He groaned. *Damn! He had ridden himself nicely into a trap!*

No time for regrets, only time – *just!* – to swing his startled, snorting mount around and head down at an angle that would take him away from the men below and those up above. All were closing in now, all shooting. Bullets whistled overhead, ricocheted from rocks, striking sparks from flintstone boulders, clattering in the dry, low-slung brush thickets.

He had a gun, didn't he? *Use the thing, you blamed fool!* he raged at himself silently and palmed up his sixgun, having sense enough to realize it would be easier to handle in the saddle than the long-barrelled Mannlicher. There was no aiming, he simply waved the gun in the general direction of the outlaws and triggered: just letting them know he was prepared to fight back. There must be at least five riders, he figured, which meant they had left at least one back at their camp to guard the senator....

The senator! What the hell was he doing when the senator had to be rescued? He was trying to save his own skin first, because, if he didn't, Senator Jay Sandlo wouldn't stand a chance of surviving. The way the rangy man had held that gun to his head, it was unlikely Sandlo was going to live for long anyway. Unless they needed him to open those chests. Well, first things first: get away from these men who were trying to kill him and *then* he could try to rescue the senator.

The thought had no sooner coursed through his mind than the dun shifted under him, jerking awkwardly, tossing its head with a half-snort, half-whinny. At once he felt the legs buckling as it started to go down. He snatched at his rifle, the foresight snagging briefly on the lip of the scabbard before ripping free, and lifted a leg over the saddle horn. He kicked away from the toppling horse and as it went downhill, skidding and kicking its last, he slammed into the slope.

Breath smashed from him and his head grazed a rock. Immediately the meteors and fireworks started again and his vision went into a swirl of out-of-focus scenes. He was rolling out of control, managed to kick against a rock and slow his slide. The impact slewed him around and he thrust wildly for a clump of low rocks. He wasn't even in behind them before the lead raked his cover and he felt a violent tug at a leg of his trousers. He worked the bolt on the Mannlicher, got off three shots before the magazine was empty or maybe a shell was hung up in the breech again. Whatever the cause, the gun wouldn't shoot and he fumbled in his pockets for the spare magazine. He couldn't find it. His head was roaring, his ears buzzing and he felt queasy again.

He blinked but couldn't bring his vision into focus. A couple of bullets whined off his cover and he sprawled face down, at the last moment remembering his sixgun. It, too, was empty and he fumbled clumsily at his belt loops for fresh cartridges. He had forgotten to work the spring-loaded rod under the barrel that punched the empty cases out of the cylinder. He dropped the few cartridges he had taken from his belt loops.

'Boys, I believe our man is either hit –or the biggest damn greenhorn ever, he's takin' so long to reload!'

It was Mace Daggett, though Kimble

didn't know that. The words reached him, but distorted and echoing, cut off, or dragged out. He thought he might have managed to get one shell into the Colt's cylinder and then heard quite clearly, the voice calling,

'Hey, feller? You all right?' That was followed by laughter. 'I believe we better go see for ourselves, boys!'

He heard boots crunch on gravel, saw hazy shapes closing in on his cover, tried to bring up his gun but it fell from his fingers. He gagged and retched and just as he slid down between the rocks, he thought:

So much for being a US marshal! Where are you now when I need you, Madigan?

He didn't know it, but Madigan and Senator Jay Sandlo were closing in on the men running up the slope. Their horses were labouring but they came in faster than the men on foot, shooting. One of the outlaws went down, rolling and skidding down the slope. Another lurched, stumbled, veered away from the rocks and hurled himself into some brush.

Mace Daggett stopped, glimpsed the horsemen coming out of the darkness, and said 'Hell with this!' He made a wild leap for some brush, crashed his way back down to where he had left his horse hitched. He was clambering frantically into the saddle, hearing the gunfire on the slope, men yelling, when another man staggered in, wild-eyed and panting. They didn't speak, wheeled their horses and spurred away out of there. A third outlaw crashed into view, running and waving his arms, shouting to him to stop and let him ride double.

Daggett rode him down and the other man triggered a shot at the sliding body. Then they were away on a mad, hurtling ride down-slope, even as the gunfire died away behind them.

There were two dead outlaws and later they found a third just inside the brushline. Madigan sat his mount, reloading both his rifle and hot sixgun. The senator was looking around, kind of startled that he had taken part in this action.

Madigan gestured to the clump of rocks where he could see part of Kimble's body sprawled.

'Best go check and see if he's still alive, Jay.'

'Huh?' Sandlo looked at him blankly for a moment and then stirred, nodding as he dismounted. 'I hope he's all right. I kind of liked that kid.'

CHAPTER 10

WILD COUNTRY

It was nearly morning before Beau Kimble started to show signs of regaining consciousness.

Madigan had the senator stand guard and keep a watch in case Daggett returned.

'Not likely he will,' Jay Sandlo said and at the marshal's quizzical look added, 'He'll probably join up with Red Roy Bissom.'

Madigan stiffened. 'Bissom's in this neck of the woods?'

The senator shrugged. 'Wouldn't swear to it but I heard Daggett talking about him. Sounded to me like he was going to meet up with him sometime. Now that we – you've – upset his plans and he's lost most of his men...'

'Yeah. Guess you're right. But keep watch anyway, Jay.'

'What the hell could've done that to the kid?'

The fire had been built up a little and the

water heated while Madigan treated Kimble's injuries. There was a large swelling above both eyes which were bruised and blackened half-way down Beau's face. One eye was swollen shut, a deep-purple shade mixing with the black. His nose was twice its normal size but didn't appear to be broken. Some of his scalp at the front had lifted a little and some hair had been torn out by the roots.

'Looks like he hit a low-hanging branch,' Madigan opined. 'Reckon he's got one helluva concussion.'

'Mightn't even know his own name.'

Madigan looked up, frowning.

'Possible. I've lost my memory temporarily after concussion. Not a good feeling.'

'But you got it back – your memory. That must've been a helluva relief.'

'You can say that again. Senator...?' Madigan pointed to the rocks. Sandlo picked up his rifle and moved off to stand guard. Then Madigan said, 'I think he's coming round.'

Sandlo was back beside him in a flash. Beau groaned and rolled his head slowly from side to side. His one good eye flickered open. Madigan spoke quietly to him, gesturing to the senator, too.

'Tracked him down. Or he tracked me

down. He got away from Daggett, anyway. You're OK now, Beau...'

Kimble was staring at Sandlo as the man leaned down towards him smiling.

'We drove off Daggett, Beau, nailed a few of his men. You recollect they were attacking you?'

Beau seemed to be thinking: his forehead was swollen too much for any kind of frown to register. Slowly, he turned his head towards Madigan. His voice was hoarse, his words halting.

'Sen-a-tor.' He gasped, rasped an unintelligible word, cleared his throat a little. 'Pr – prisoner...?'

Jay Sandlo chuckled, patted Beau's shoulder.

'No need to make it into a question, Beau. If you saw me in Daggett's camp, you know I was his prisoner. Hell, he threatened to blow my head off when I baulked at...' He stopped, flicked his gaze to Madigan, shrugged. 'Guess we better not overload him right away, huh?'

'Be best not to,' Madigan agreed slowly. 'Look, Jay, how about you take Beau on down to the doctor, get him seen to? I reckon the sooner he gets medical attention the better.'

'Yes, I s'pose so. But what're you going to do?'

'Go after Daggett. That's my next priority now you're OK. I can tell you how to get down to the trail...'

'Be best if you drew me a rough map, Bronco.'

'All right.' He turned to Beau Kimble. 'You hear all that?'

But Beau had passed out again. Madigan took out a small black, leather-covered notebook and pencil stub and began to sketch in the trail out of the Nightshades.

'First time I've been this far into 'em, so you'll have to use your discretion if I don't have the map quite right. Generally keep in a south-west direction after you cross the river.'

Sandlo nodded absently as he took the map, looking at Kimble.

'He doesn't look so good.'

'Sooner you get him down there the better.'

Still the senator hesitated.

'How'll you know where to go after Daggett?'

'Tracks, when it gets a little lighter. But one thing about that damn deskwork – and the files. They keep them right up to date.

144

Bissom was last heard of up around Yankton, so if he's got a rendezvous with Daggett he'll be coming south which means Daggett'll be going north to meet him. I know Bissom and Daggett rode together a few years back, holed up in a snakes' nest of canyons south-west of the Winnebago Reservation, out towards Wisner. You work around the Nightshades you'll come out into Winnebago country. Daggett can follow the river into those canyons then.'

'Where you reckon he hung out with Bissom before? Bit of a long shot, Bronco.'

'Long shots are all I've got.'

'But he'll have a good lead, most of the night. You won't catch him in time. Hell, man, just think of the odds.'

Madigan pointed to the mountains. 'I'll go up and over.'

Senator Jay Sandlo looked horrified.

'Kerrriiiist! You'll kill your horse!'

'It can be done. And has been. Fact, it was Daggett who did it, staying one jump ahead of a Wells Fargo posse.'

'Then why won't he try it this time?'

Madigan smiled thinly. 'He just might.'

Then the senator shook his head, smiling ruefully.

'You son of a gun. That's what you're

hoping, ain't it? Put you closer to him, let him get over the rim, and pick him off from the high country.'

'It's a chance.'

'Don't take too many of them, Bronco. Don't push your luck.'

'Best way to use luck – if you've got any.'

Madigan's plan almost worked. Except his packhorse gave up the ghost before they topped-out on the ridge. The animal had been struggling for the last hour and Madigan had called a reluctant halt to allow it to recuperate. Obviously it wasn't enough. The horse had fought and squealed and tugged wildly at the knotted link-rope and in the end had actually pulled Madigan clear out of the saddle. He held on to his end of the rope and was dragged ten yards downslope before the packhorse's legs folded and he sat down and wouldn't – or couldn't move another inch.

Madigan took his saddle canteen, punched a hollow in his hat-crown and spilled some water into it. The panting animal drank gratefully. Then he unloaded his gear, removed bridle and pack-frames. By then the horse was able to stand and with a snort and a last biting lunge at the marshal by way of goodbye, took off in an awkward sliding run downslope.

Madigan swore mildly, gathered his grub sacks and whatever else he could carry in reasonable comfort and returned to the waiting sorrel. Its ears were pricked as it watched the packhorse disappearing into the brush.

'Don't get any ideas!' Madigan growled as he loaded his gear. 'You and me've got a long way to go yet, *amigo.*'

The sorrel took him to the crest of the ridge, but only just made it up the steep incline. It was blowing, froth-caked, the yellowish foam sliding down quivering legs and slopping from the withers. Madigan was short of breath, too. He had dismounted the last twenty yards and dragged and heaved, used his shoulder, digging in his boots, legs a-quiver, helping the horse over the last steep yards.

They both rested on top and he swallowed some water, gave the sorrel a drink out of his battered hat. Then he took his field glasses and scanned the country below. Within a couple of minutes he knew one of two things had happened.

He had guessed wrong – or Daggett and

his man had outdistanced him and were now deep in the heavy, darkening woods down below.

Either way, for now he had lost them.

He decided to make camp on the ridge, see if he could spot their camp-fire when night fell – which wasn't too far away, for it had taken most of the day to make his way up this side of the mountain. Still, shorter than going the long way round, although more exhausting.

Once again he ate cold grub and washed it down with canteen water. He would need to refill as early as possible tomorrow. He spent the last hours of daylight making himself a snug camp amongst boulders, sliding and slipping down to the timberline and cutting some pine branches to roof his shelter. He would be comfortable this night, but he sat shivering outside with his jacket laced all the way to his throat, gloves on his hands, making it awkward to adjust the field glasses as he tracked them over the woods below.

Once he thought he saw a yellow glow almost directly below but when he looked away for a moment to rest his eyes, he thought he saw another glow that could be a small camp-fire or even a man smoking more to the left. Then it rose slowly, slowly and he reckoned, yeah, it was a man having a cigarette all right. But then the point of light lifted and dropped, apparently tied itself in a bow, shot in a straight line, first right, then left.

'Goddamn fireflies!' he said bitterly.

He watched for another hour and by then it was full dark and his hands were numb and his teeth were chattering. But just before he ducked into his shelter and hurriedly climbed into his bedroll, he caught a whiff of something that brought a thin smile to his face.

A faint tang of woodsmoke, drifting up from below.

They were down there, all right, likely far ahead of him, hiding their fire, but he was on the right track.

He slept warm and well and rose to a frosty dawn, rewarded by seeing a thin tendril of blueish smoke way out in the trees down there, a lot further out than he had reckoned on. He would have some making-up to do today if he wanted to catch Daggett.

The wind was blowing away from Daggett's camp, so Madigan built himself a fire and luxuriated in its warmth, made hot coffee, then went all the way now that he knew where his quarry was – roughly – and fried up some sowbelly and beans and crumbled a couple of stale biscuits into the fat in the skillet. Washed down with the last of the coffee, the food made him feel way better.

Until he heard the gunshot....

It came from downslope, *his* slope, and he crouched behind a big boulder, rifle in gloved hands as he scanned the brush and trees below. There were two more shots, close together, and he swore, hoping the sound wouldn't carry up and over to where the outlaws were. He didn't think it would, but it was just possible, even with the wind blowing the wrong way. The shots sounded like a signal, something to get a man's attention.

'Who the hell is it?' he asked himself aloud and then straightened, rifle coming to his shoulder as he saw movement down below at the edge of the brush.

He swore again as the man down there made a sweeping motion with his arm, indicating that he wanted Madigan to come down to him.

It was Senator Jay Sandlo.

And he was in a right state by the time Madigan reached him, angry and sweating from the effort of sliding and tumbling down the mountain.

'What the hell're you doing here?' Madigan demanded, panting. Then he looked past the senator and asked, 'Where's the kid?'

'That's why I came back. Your map was wrong. We took a sharp turn in a trail and it put us right above the river which is running like an express train. Heavy rain back in the hills or canyon country, I guess.'

'What the hell're you saying?'

Jay Sandlo looked levelly at Madigan, his face set stiffly.

'I'm saying the kid went in – rode clear off the bank or the edge crumbled or something, but one way or another, Beau went into that river and him and his horse were gone in the blink of an eye. Thought I'd best come and tell you. Almost rode my own mount into the ground, doing it.'

Madigan stared at the upset senator, then swore briefly.

'We better go look.'

'Hell. Bronco, no one could survive long enough to even call for help in that wild water!'

'We'll have to look. He could've got hung up on a sandbank or a snag. It's worth a try.'

Sandlo frowned. 'Thought you didn't like the kid.' Madigan gave him a brittle look. 'What's that got to do with it? I'm responsible for him.'

The senator stared back for a long moment, then spread his hands, shrugging.

'If you want the hassle of climbing way back up there to collect your mount, ride it down here and then all the way out to the river...'

'When it's your sidekick, Jay, it's no trouble. Thought you might remember that.'

As the marshal turned away and began the long climb to where he had left his mount, Jay Sandlo nodded slowly, mouth tight.

Sure he remembered. A place called Bootleg Bend. Jay Sandlo had taken a Yankee ball in the ribs and was coughing blood. He and Madigan were separated from the rest of the troop in really wild country. They had no water or food, very little ammunition, most of their powder was damp and their few percussion caps were mangled from a fall they had taken into a deep crevice.

And they were a long way from their own lines.

Madigan had carried him over his back, holding both their rifles in one hand, a Gunnison & Griswald copy of a Colt pistol in his other, with only two loads in the cylinder. Jay was mostly delirious and shouted once in a while. Twice Madigan had slugged him unconscious when they were hiding while Yankee patrols passed along narrow trails, only yards from where they crouched. Then they came to the creek, just after dark, and Madigan's legs were like rubber, his spine cracking, muscles screaming in pain.

Madigan laid out Jay Sandlo on the only blanket they had between them and shook him.

'Stay quiet. There's a Yankee patrol camped on the far bank. I'm going over, get you some medicine and proper bandages. I'll grab grub and ammo if I can....'

Suffering severe pain, afraid he was dying, Jay had feebly grabbed his arm.

'Too much of a – hassle, Bren. You – you'll get caught – or drown. You must be plumb tuckered.'

'I've been worse.' He squeezed Jay's arm.

'Smother them coughs when you feel 'em coming on. I'll be back.'

And he was. Jay Sandlo had no idea how long Madigan took but when he awoke, his wound was being bandaged with proper army calico strips and it felt better, yet raw.

'Washed it with antiseptic and sprinkled it with boracic powder,' Madigan told him. 'Got a whole medical kit here. You'll be OK, Jay. We'll get back to our lines eventually.'

'You – have any trouble?'

'Little. Had to kill the sentry. Ran a bayonet into him from behind...'

'Owe you – Bren – Never forget this...'

'You survive and we can both forget it...'

Yeah – both forget it. Well, Sandlo hadn't ever really forgotten it – but had forgotten the unwritten code that Madigan lived by: never abandon a pardner or sidekick until you see him dead. Then you give him a damn good burial before leaving....

Sandlo didn't know if he would be capable of that, staying around in enemy territory just to bury a dead man.

They arrived at the river mid-morning and it was really racing, though Madigan could see it had dropped quite a few inches, going by the flattened grass and wash-aways above the level of the broken, muddy water.

He found where Beau's horse had stepped too close to the crumbly edge and it had given way. He mounted a rock and scanned the banks as far as he could see, then climbed down, shaking his head at Sandlo's enquiring look.

'Nothing.'

The senator licked his lips, then turned

154

and pointed at a small cove just before the next bend.

'Thought I caught a glimpse of something blue over there. Might be a wildflower but... Beau was wearing a blue shirt, wasn't he?'

'Believe he was...'

'Come up here beside me. You can just see it.'

Madigan stepped up and the senator grabbed his arm, pointing. 'Might have to lean out a little. I'll hold you. Line up that tree branch in the water with the balsam fir on the far bank...'

Madigan lifted to his toes, straining to see, leaning out, steadied by Jay Sandlo.

Then suddenly Jay's grip slackened and Madigan let out a yell as he plunged towards the roaring water.

Sandlo said, 'Sorry, Bronco...' And just as Madigan splashed in and the river closed over his head, he heard the crack of a rifle from across the river.

A distinctive sound. The kind a Mannlicher rifle makes.

CHAPTER 11

WILD RIVER

The water rushed down his throat and he closed his mouth swiftly, gagging, coughing, arms thrashing as he fought to the surface. *Surface? Which way was that?*

He was tumbling wildly, kicked and buffeted and thrown about by worse than the meanest bronc he had ever ridden. He spun and, half-way through the spin, was wrenched back the other way, head down, then head up, but before he could gulp in a lungful of air, he was sucked down again, jostled and punched and *trampled* as if he was caught in a stampede. It was only an illusion, the trampling – it was his body banging and bouncing off a succession of rocks of various shapes and sizes, from a man's fist to twice the size of a human head. His senses were awhirl and his eyes felt as if they were rolling in his head, being prised out of their sockets.

Then he glimpsed light, like a yellow patch

of lamp-glow showing through a fog-hazed window in a mountain cabin. Instinctively, he kicked up and thrust with his arms. His head broke through and he glimpsed a bouncing jigsaw of images, too fast for them to coalesce into a single picture.

An instant later it seemed as if the world had fallen in and landed on his shoulders.

There was a tremendous weight smashing on top of him, driving him deep into the river, crushing him. He struck bottom and clunking rocks rolled across his ribs like an opponent's riding-boots. His left arm struck hard and he thought it was broken. Lights burst behind his eyes. He was briefly stretched out on the bottom, flattened by the huge, convulsing, thrashing weight above him. His ribs creaked.

Muddy water roared about him as it churned and bubbled. Grit stirred and stung his flesh, blinded him even more than he was already. There was a feeling like a woman's hair dragging across his face and he snatched at it instinctively. He was yanked violently upwards and even as he realized he was hanging on to a horse's mane, they burst through the surface.

The river had them. It was his own sorrel, eyes rolling wildly, white with fear, teeth bared, water gurgling down its throat so that its frightened whinny sounded more like bathwater going down the drain. Madigan snatched at the arched neck, got one arm around the wet hide and clung tightly. They were wrenched and whirled away, spinning on the surface, the clouds above streaking across the sky. Deep water surrounded them then and both man and horse kicked wildly, legs scissoring and scrabbling for a grip that wasn't there.

The river held them and spun them, having its way with them. They were helpless and Madigan somehow cleared his vision long enough to see, fifty yards or more upstream, Senator Jay Sandlo, lashing at his horse with his rein ends, kicking its flanks frantically, as he fought it away from the crumbly bank of the river.

The man got it going and disappeared behind the rocks. Something puffed and spurted dust from the boulders, a second eruption following quickly. Then the senator was gone and Madigan was fighting to pick up the sorrel's trailing reins. He got them, wrapped the wet leather about his left forearm, clinging to the mane with his other hand.

The banks blurred past. Then the current

abruptly nudged them to its very edge where a sandbank turned the deep water in a tight U and briefly aimed it at the far bank. He took this in in a flash, hurled his sodden body against the still frightened horse, although it had calmed some with the familiar tug of the bridle on its mouth and the weight of the man on the reins. Madigan hooked an arm over the saddle horn, kicked and used his knees against the horse's side, turning it slightly as the current carried them along the edge of the sandbank, before it reversed direction.

The horse flailed its legs, searching for purchase, ready to lunge up on to the bank. That was the thing Madigan didn't want it to do: that would get them out of the water, sure, but they would still be stranded in the middle of the river on the bank which was awash, knee-deep.

Madigan wanted out of the river altogether.

He punched the horse in the throat, chewed on one ear until he had its attention and it gave up trying to fight him so it could reach the relative safety of the sandbank.

'Good! Good!' he gasped. 'Now make for the other bank.'

As he spoke, he slid into the saddle, not worrying about getting his boots into the stirrups which were flailing about in the white-capped water. The sorrel seemed happier to have him on its back again, to be under his control, him giving the orders. Madigan leaned over the stretching neck and spoke quietly into the laid-back ears, kicking the flanks, urging the horse to swim towards the bank opposite to where he had fallen in, and now only twenty feet away.

The currents were wild, splashing into waves, slapping the sorrel in the face and making it toss its head. It smacked the marshal in the face and he saw spinning bright lights and felt warm blood trickling from his nostrils.

'Go, you jughead! *Go!*'

The horse was close enough to smell the vegetation on the bank now and it made an effort, no longer fighting him, just swimming across the currents, guided at an angle by the rider. In five minutes it was heaving up and out of the river. Madigan slid from the saddle and sank to his knees on the grass, gripping a handful as if to reassure himself he was back on solid ground. The horse shook itself, spraying silver, then wandered on to a deep green patch and began to browse.

Madigan hung his head, breathing deeply, feeling his pounding heart settle, trying to get his brain into gear so he could work out what had happened.

Kimble! It had been Kimble's rifle that had fired back there and the bullet had either struck the senator or passed close enough to startle him so that he loosened his hold on Madigan – and as a result, the marshal fell into the river. When he had surfaced with the horse, which must have been frightened by the shooting and jumped or fallen in the river, too, Madigan had seen bullets kicking dust from the boulders. So the kid had been *still* shooting all the time he had been submerged. What the hell was going on? Jay Sandlo had said Kimble had been snatched away by the raging current. So what the hell was Kimble doing *across* the river, shooting at the senator?

The bushes rustled beyond the browsing horse and the sorrel raised its head, ears pricking. Madigan, still shaking from his exertions, fumbled as he went to draw his Colt. Then he froze as he heard a rifle bolt clash and Beau T. Kimble appeared out of the brush, bandage gone from his head, clothes wet and ragged, staring at him out of a pair of deep blackened sockets, his eyes looking almost. . . mad.

He was also covering Madigan with his

Mannlicher rifle.

'What're you playing at, kid?' Madigan gasped, lifting his hands out from his sides. 'Why're you trying to kill the senator?'

'I can't see well enough to shoot straight yet, so I wasn't really trying to kill him. I just wanted to drive him off and give you a chance to survive the river.'

It didn't make sense to Madigan but he said:

'Like you did?'

'I was lucky, Bronco. He rammed his horse into mine, put us both into the river – it was even rougher and deeper than it is now. We went under but I never lost my grip on the reins. I haven't been able to see properly since I hit that tree-branch. It scared me and I wrapped the reins around my forearms, hung on as tight as I could. I guess we were whipped away mighty fast, around the bend or somewhere on the far side of the sandbank. In any case, out of the senator's sight. We eventually got to shore on this side and I must've passed out. When I came round, I started upstream, simply because that's the way the horse seemed to want to go. Then I saw you and the senator arrive and when he got you up on that rock he took your arm while you leaned out. I knew he was going to push you in. I fired a shot near him, hoping I wouldn't hit you, trying to startle him, tell him I'm alive.'

'Kid! Your shot gave him such a start he let go my arm. I *fell* in. He didn't push me.'

It was hard to read the expression on Kimble's battered face but there was anger in his voice.

'He tried to murder you – the way he did me! He must've thought I was long dead by the time he got back with you, don't you see?'

'Yeah, he thought you'd drowned. He said he searched but couldn't find you, then came to fetch me.'

'He didn't make any search for me! He rode away and left me. He *meant* me to drown.'

'Now why would he do that?'

Kimble was silent for a short time.

'Because – because I'd seen him in Mace Daggett's camp, Mace holding a gun to his head while he tried to make him open the locks on the two chests...'

That made Madigan take notice.

'What chests?'

'The two iron-bound chests Daggett and his men brought back with them. Cash boxes, I'd say, but with funny-looking locks. I couldn't see properly but they looked like *round* padlocks, very thick metal.'

'Combination padlocks,' Madigan said only half-aloud. 'The army sometimes uses them on express boxes, impossible to open unless you know the right combination.' He snapped his head up. 'But Jay never mentioned any chests to me. And why would Daggett think the senator knew how to open them? Or are you saying that's why Daggett took him prisoner in the first place?'

Kimble curled a purple lip.

'He wasn't a prisoner. He had the run of the camp.'

'What?' Madigan was very tense now, watching closely.

'I thought he was a prisoner at first but afterwards when my headache started to fade, I thought about it some more. He'd walked down from that cave without any bonds. Talking and smiling at the man who was with him.'

'You said Daggett held a gun to his head.'

'He did. But I think Daggett was drunk, if not with actual booze, just on the fact that he had brought back the chests successfully. I thought he was going to shoot the senator and was sighting in my rifle when a guard I hadn't seen jumped me. But just before he did, Daggett lowered his gun, clapped the senator on the back and laughed – as if it had all been one big joke.'

Madigan was silent. It had bothered him that there had been no rope-burns on Jay Sandlo's wrists. And there was no bump on the man's head that he could see, sure no broken skin as there would be if he had been slugged with a gun butt as Fern Pascale had claimed.

Maybe that story had been just for Madigan's benefit. Which meant that Senator Jay Sandlo had gone willingly with Mace Daggett, wanted outlaw, infamous train robber, killer...

News of the train robbery at Buckwheat Bridge where the chests were stolen had reached Madigan before he came north. *Seemed the outlaws knew just where to look for them, too, behind that sham wall panel...*

'But why the hell would a Washington senator team up with a gang of outlaws?'

He had spoken aloud and Kimble, now sitting on the grass beside the marshal, rifle still held in his hands but no longer threatening, said:

'I think he's been in on the railroad robberies all along.'

Madigan's stare was quick and appraising.

'Now what would give you such a notion?

I've known Jay Sandlo for over twenty years. We went through the War together, and we've hunted many a deer and mountain lion since. He likes a high time and he's something of a curly wolf under that senator's image he puts on, but he's no train robber...'

'Well, he doesn't have to be. Daggett and Bissom do the actual robbing. And the occasional wrecking. All Sandlo has to do is tell them when. And where.'

'Such as when the trains are carrying express boxes or valuable freight?'

Kimble nodded. 'It's part of the senator's job to approve applications for railroad right-of-ways and make sure they're going to be profitable and not fold up after a few months. So he has to know all about their profits and losses and generally cultivate the men who own the railroads. Just as they do the same with him, scratching each others' backs. He moves in the right circles for that – as does my father on occasions.'

He added this last quietly and in a different tone from the rest of what he had said. His still-swollen eyes held steadily to Madigan's face.

'Your – father?'

'Yeah. He has shares in several railroads. Looking for leverage for when it comes time for them to lay tracks down our way and for the shipping of our herds...'

'Go on,' Madigan said quietly, gaze steady.

'Well, the senator kept hammering the point that he liked to give his constituents their money's-worth, that he wouldn't use public money for his own hunting-trips or just visit anywhere that wouldn't produce some worthwhile results. It made me – well, it *irritated* me. There was too much of his being such an upright politician. I knew you and Marshal Parminter thought very highly of him but I reckoned it mightn't hurt to get – an outside opinion.'

'Like your father's?'

Kimble smiled thinly.

'You're getting ahead of me, Bronco! Yes. On the way to Omaha Jay kept telling me what a wonderful marriage he had – then he went out and picked up that Fern woman. When we went hunting and paid off the guide because he didn't live up to expectations, he gave him a pay-chit, told him to take it to the nearest railroad administration offices and he would get his money. This from a man who was making so much of the fact that he never used any money but his own for such trips. So I wired Dad to find out what he could about our wonderful senator.'

'Just stick with the facts, kid,' Madigan growled.

'Well, before I left Omaha to look for Sandlo, Dad's wire came.' He paused and seemed to think about his next words before continuing: 'Jay Sandlo has shares in every railroad that he's approved for building.'

'That's illegal. Vested interest.'

'Which is why he put the shares in his wife's name, I suppose.'

'I think that's still illegal – but why would he condone the railroads being robbed if he has shares in them?'

Kimble's smile widened.

'Because a series of robberies will shake the faith of people who want to use the railroads for shipping their goods.'

'Kid, you lost me.'

'Think about it, Bronco. Without backing from the public, railroad profits fall, shares drop in value...'

'It's just another reason why Jay *wouldn't* get involved in the robberies.'

'Buy shares at a low price, sell at a high. Men make hundreds of thousands of dollars that way, Bronco.'

Madigan frowned.

'That's a gamble. No one can be sure if share prices will rise ... or fall.'

'Unless you're the man to approve track routes and government shipping via rail *and* express freight. Then you can be tolerably sure ... pretty *damn* sure, as a matter of fact. And if you get the robberies cleaned up after you've bought up a stack of low-price shares, everything goes sky-high and you make a mighty big profit.'

'Yeah, kid, you could just have something.' Madigan stood. 'Except I don't believe, a word of it. Jay Sandlo would never get mixed up in anything like that.'

'How d'you know, Bronco? You said it's been years since you've seen him. You don't know what might've happened to push him into something like this.'

Madigan's face was harder than Beau Kimble had ever seen it.

'I knew you were gonna be a burr under my saddle soon as I saw you, kid.'

Kimble flushed, and curled a lip.

'Yeah, well I should've known you wouldn't believe the senator rode anything but a white horse.'

Madigan raked him with a cold stare.

'Your theory is something that might work, kid. It just won't fit Jay Sandlo, is all. Why would he come to the Marshals and ask for me to ride shotgun with him? Look into the train robberies? He knows how I work, that once I get my teeth into something, I don't let go...'

'You've answered your own question.'

Madigan blinked and the kid hitched around, sounding excited now.

'You clear up the robberies, and, as you say, he knows how you work. So he wouldn't expect you to bring in any of the outlaws still alive. If by some miracle you did, he'd be there to make sure the man didn't talk...'

It stopped Madigan: the kid had an answer to everything.

And, just to rub it in, Beau added:

'Then the railroads would have the public's confidence again, and the shares would rise, and–'

Madigan held up a hand.

'All right! You've got it all figured. It's out of my field, but I can see what you're getting at. I just can't bring myself to believe it.'

'Well, I can't *make* you believe it, but–'

'We'll go ask the senator,' Madigan said curtly, stretching the kinks out of his aching limbs. 'Saddle up.'

CHAPTER 12

WILD MEN

Red Roy Bissom didn't have red hair. He had a red face and that was the source of his nickname.

It was something to do with permanently inflamed blood vessels just under the skin and was a constant embarrassment to him. Actually, he'd grown used to it over the years – he had had the condition most of his life – but he saw the way people looked at him when they saw him for the first time, how some of them stepped wide in case it was some sort of disease that was catching. That upset him and he showed it in bad temper, earned a reputation for being one of the meanest sons of bitches ever to ride the Dakota owlhoot trails.

But now he was down in Nebraska, with his two best gunfighters, Kiley and Oakes, waiting not too patiently at the rendezvous where they were supposed to be met by Mace Daggett and his bunch.

'Two riders comin', Roy,' Kiley said from where he sat on a deadfall, looking down the valley trail. Kiley was a stretched-out man with a face like a horse and a temperament that damn near matched Bissom's. Kiley's problem was he was so skinny that sometimes town kids followed him down the street, calling:

'Want to know the way to the undertaker's, mister? You look dead and just ain't gotten around to lyin' down yet!'

He'd kicked many a kid's skinny butt in patched pants – and gotten himself into fights over it, too. Last time he'd killed a woman, the kid's mother, he thought. Hadn't meant to, but what it did mean was that he had to stay away from towns for quite some time. You didn't go around killing women, not even on the wide-open Dakota frontier.

'*Two* riders?' Bissom growled, taking the hat off his face where it had rested while he dozed against a big pine. 'Ought to be at least six. Might've left a man to guard his camp but...'

He was standing now, shading his eyes as he looked down the winding trail. Kiley had his rifle cocked and Oakes was standing, hand on the butt of his holstered sixgun.

'Yeah. Looks like Mace, all right,' Bissom said slowly, sniffing: that was another thing that embarrassed him, Part of whatever had caused his red face left him with chronic sniffles, usually worse in the morning, but a big dewy drop could form on the end of his knife-blade nose at just about any time. He wiped the back of a hairy wrist across it irritably now, blinking – another damn annoying symptom. All that was left was for him to go into a fit of sneezing....

'Goddamnit! He shouldn't have even thought about it! He sneezed violently – at least a dozen times, hawked and cursed bitterly and by then Daggett and his man, Hood, were riding up the slope.

'Hey, Roy! Heard you sniffin' way down-trail. Just waited for the sneezin' to start.' Mace Daggett grinned. 'Knew it was you then so I leathered my gun.'

'You better keep it in your damn hand you gonna smart-talk me that way!' Bissom growled.

Daggett's smile widened.

'Feelin' a mite bloody today, Roy? Well, I can savvy that.' The smile faded slowly as he indicated Hood. 'All that's left of the boys – and Splinter who I left in camp with the senator.'

175

'Sandlo? We gotta deal with him?'

'No other way. He's gonna make us rich, Roy,' Daggett said, dismounting stiffly, pressing his hands into the small of his back and arching his spine. 'Damn! That feels good! Yeah. We pulled that robbery of the ore train. You mighta heard about it?'

Bissom frowned. 'An *ore* train? The hell you want to hold up one of them for? Couple thousand tons of rock. Gonna build a castle or somethin'?'

'Roy, you gotta stay in touch more. No, that ore train was carryin' gold, *amigo*. Two chests hid behind a false partition in the caboose. Senator knew about it, likely arranged it.' Daggett suddenly scowled. 'Tried to get him to open 'em but he said he couldn't. I was sorta joshin' and put a gun to his head, kinda playin' with him a bit, but I think I really scared him. But he wouldn't back down. Said *you* were the one that could open 'em.'

All three men were watching Bissom now, saw him blink several times, the genuine surprise washing over his fiery face.

'Me?'

'That's what he said.' Daggett spoke flatly, eyes boring into Bissom now.

'Why the hell didn't you just shoot the locks off?'

176

'Couldn't. Tried it, matter of fact, before we took the chests back to the senator. Helluva tough locks, queer ones, too. Dangling short, with very thick bodies and a sorta little knob or wheel in front, ringed by numbers.'

Bissom stiffened. 'Combination locks!'

'That's what the senator said. Reckons you know the numbers.'

He was expecting Bissom to bluster and ask how the hell *he* would know, but the red face, although it darkened a little, lifted and Bissom raked them with – watery eyes.

'How old're these chests?'

'I dunno. Few years, I'd say. Iron-bound, but got some rust on 'em, though the bands are mighty thick. Wood's sheathed in iron, too. Take a bundle of dynamite to even crack 'em, I reckon.'

'You got these off an *ore* train?'

'What's the matter, Roy? All them sniffles and the sneezin' affectin' your hearin'?'

Bissom narrowed his eyes and thinned-out his lips. But he could see Daggett was on the edge, too, having lost some of his men – and he hadn't yet said *how*. There was no point in forcing this. Leastways, not until he found out just what was happening.

There were wild thoughts whirling about

177

in his head but he wasn't sure just how much to ask – he could give it away if he asked the wrong question. Still, he needed to know.

'Reckon those chests could be twenty years old, thereabouts?'

Daggett frowned, not yet relaxing, not trusting Bissom's meanness: the man might just lull him into a state of trust and then suddenly blow him in two. But Red Roy sure did seem puzzled.

'Might be. Rust on 'em like I said. Look like they'd been buried.'

Bissom straightened suddenly.

'What?' Daggett demanded, the others watching closely. 'What's in them chests, Roy? Whatever it is, it near breaks the back of two men to handle one chest.' He didn't wait for Bissom to answer. 'I reckon only thing that heavy would be gold. But it was the train from the lead mine.'

'They the ones diggin' out near Pig's Eye Butte?'

'Been workin' that country for years. I hear they're actually tunnellin' *into* the base of the butte now. Why?' He asked this when he saw Bissom's head begin to nod.

Now the red-faced outlaw looked up and bared his teeth, not even bothering to wipe away the next dewdrop that had formed on the end of his nose. Just before he started to sneeze, he said:

'They damn well found it! Musta been a thousand to one chance! Diggin' for lead and find – gold.'

A vicious bout of sneezing prevented him adding any more right then and when he had finished hawking and sniffing, wiping his eyes and nose with a kerchief, he looked around at Daggett and the others.

'You know I fought with the Yankees durin' the War.'

'So did I,' said Hood, and Riley nodded but whether he was admitting to the same thing or not he didn't say out loud.

'Just before the end, I was transferred to a special troop that had to deliver six chests of gold bars to General Augustus Claire at Minneapolis.'

'That Yankee butcher!' breathed Daggett.

'Butcher or not, he whipped your Reb asses back south and he was headed for Washington for some kind of award from Lincoln himself when someone decided he'd be the man to escort in the six chests of Confederate gold bars we'd took in a raid. The officers didn't trust us, sheathed the chests in iron, put on them special combination locks. They was new, came from Europe, and some of the war-backers over there – in the arms trade mostly – got 'em for our men. Only one man knew the combinations. Our officer, name of Dally, walkin' ramrod, Reb-hater from way back.'

'I heard of him. Had a special camp one time where they tortured Johnny Rebs...'

Bissom nodded. 'Cut the story short... There was a bunch of Reb raiders on the loose, hittin' and runnin' anythin' that smelled of Yankees. They somehow got on to what we were doin'. Our outriders started gettin' picked off, one by one, and that scared Dally – figured they were after him. We made a run, lost the Rebs for a spell, and Dally said we'd bury the gold in three different places. I wasn't on that detail but we all knew roughly where they hid 'em. Fact, a few of us went back after the war but no one found anythin' far as I heard. Know damn well *I* didn't.'

'You're sayin', these chests we took from the ore train are part of that gold stash?' Daggett's eyes were bulging a little.

'Could be. We knew some was buried out near Pig's Eye. But we run into Injuns, see, and there was a helluva fight, chased us for miles, wanted our ammo and guns. Just about wiped us out. I was with a small group with Dally and he was hit bad. We got separated and I was stuck with him. He knew he wasn't gonna make it, give me a little notebook, said the combinations of the locks were in there. Wanted me to get on through to General Claire, turn over the book and started to tell me where the chests were buried but died on the spot.' He snapped his fingers. 'Just like that, middle of a word – and the word was "pig". Didn't take much to work out he was going to say "Pig's Eye".'

They waited for more but Bissom smiled, built a cigarette, and as he fumbled for a match just said:

''Course, I'd give my word I'd get the book through to General Claire.'

'You still got the book?' Daggett asked hoarsely.

Bissom shook his head. He looked up through the smoke and tapped his temple.

'In here. Got a good memory.'

'You couldn't remember a bunch of numbers for more'n twenty years!' Daggett made no attempt to hide his scepticism.

'Well, you show me them chests and if I can work out which ones they are out of the six, I'll open 'em. Provided the locks still work.'

'Oh, they'll work all right – might need a

181

little oil but they'll work. They were made by Swiss watchmakers.'

The men jumped as a bedraggled Senator Jay Sandlo came out of the trees on foot. He lifted a hand as they reached for their guns.

'Relax, gents. First we have to go back to where the chests are.'

'Hell! You left 'em lyin' in the open at the camp?' Daggett said – actually only remembering now that they had abandoned the chests when they had gone after Kimble.

The senator smiled thinly.

'Not exactly. Splinter helped me move them.'

'Yeah, well where is Splinter anyway?'

'He had an – accident. But only after we had put the chests in a safe place.'

'And that was where?'

'Right now, Mace, I'm the only man alive who knows where.' He flicked his eyes to Bissom who was staring at him bleakly. 'Howdy, Roy. Long time since we tied one on in Deadwood, eh?'

'May twenty-fourth, eighteen-eighty-one,' Bissom said without hesitation.

'You've got a good memory! I recall you cried in your beer about what a hard life you'd had with that face of yours and how you could be a rich man – if only you knew just where that rebel gold was buried.'

Bissom curled a lip.

'I've never been that drunk since! You poured that lousy red-eye into me! I was never sure just how much I'd told you.'

'Enough. Enough so that when the people who run the lead mine sent word to my office – by mistake, you see – it should have gone to "Minerals and Natural Wealth" but I head a committee that's supposed to watch that mining and tree-felling and railroads don't ruin good grazing land, and the message wound up on my desk. It said that during mining operations they had unearthed two old iron-bound chests with strange locks that were impossible to open – what should they do with them?'

'Hell! It was just an accident they found 'em?'

Sandlo spread his hands.

'Looks that way. I told them to ship them on one of their ore trains, in a secure manner, which I described, and said I'd take care of them.' He glanced at Daggett. 'Mace picked 'em up and now all we have to do is open them. Over to you, Roy. You feeling up to it?'

Bissom met and held his mocking gaze.

'You show me the chests, I'll open 'em.'

'Fine. Oh, one other thing, gents. Madigan's somewhere along my backtrail. With that new sidekick of his. Why, gents, how come each and every one of you has suddenly gone all grey? You look positively *sick!*'

'Why'd you want to bring that son of a bitch, anyway?' demanded Bissom.

Jay Sandlo smiled.

'I figured he could track you down and bring you in. Didn't know Mace had already made a rendezvous with you. So, now I don't need Madigan any more.'

Red Roy Bissom raked his gaze around at the men and set his watery eyes levelly on Sandlo's face.

'No,' he said heavily. 'Just me.'

184

CHAPTER 13

HIDEOUT OR GRAVEYARD?

'We're not going to make it up and over the range with these jugheads.'

Madigan leaned on his saddle horn, then sat back, hooked a boot over and took out the makings. As he built the cigarette he watched Kimble on top of his jaded horse, patting its neck as he leaned forward slightly and scanned the steep slope. *Point to you, kid,* Madigan allowed silently as the young marshal continued to gentle his weary mount.

'We don't go up, what can we do? Take the long way round?' the kid asked, looking worried.

'Only two ways. Up and over, or the long way.' Madigan fired-up, offered the tobacco sack to Kimble who shook his head.

'They'll be too far ahead if we go round, Bronco. We'll never catch up.'

Madigan nodded, 'Mebbe we should go somewhere else.'

The kid looked startled.

'What does that mean? We can't give up now!'

Point two to you, Beau, old amigo!

'Those chests will be mighty heavy. If you're right about the senator, he couldn't've moved them by himself at that camp. He told me he got away from someone named Splinter whom Mace left behind to watch him. The two of 'em might've stashed the chests someplace back there. Wouldn't be far, because of the weight.'

Kimble frowned. 'What you're saying is that when Mace rendezvous with Bissom – if that's what he's doing – they'll go back to Daggett's hideout to work on the chests?'

Madigan nodded, drew deep on his smoke.

'And you want us to be waiting for them?'

'What d'you think?'

Kimble actually jerked in the saddle: it was the first time Madigan had asked for his opinion about anything.

'Well ... good idea. But how many men might Bissom have with him?'

'That's the joker in the pack. I'm pretty damn sure Bissom won't be alone.'

'Uh-huh. But s'pose they just meet up and take off to pull another job somewhere else?'

'Chance we take. But I don't think so. Bissom isn't your usual outlaw.'

186

Beau frowned. 'From what I read in the files he's just a mean-eyed scum who enjoys killing.'

'He has a red face. Some condition with his blood vessels. He's had to put up with a helluva lot of joshing over the years and it's turned him real mean. But he's had some education. The story is he started out working in his father's store in Boston, handled all the bookwork. Then one day he suddenly broke loose, killed his elder brother for something he said about his face, burned the store and the family home and lit out for the owlhoot.'

'Sounds like the makings of a typical outlaw to me.'

Madigan shook his head.

'Not so. The Service medico told me one time that men like Bissom with a physical affliction will find some way to compensate. Like a man with no legs will become mighty good at doing things with his hands, not just pulling himself around, but delicate things – maybe writing books, painting pictures, fixing clocks – things that don't matter how many legs a man has or hasn't.'

'Yes, I understand. I have a cousin who has something wrong with his spine, all warped and shuffles around like a spider.

But, man, can he cook! Not just meat and stuff, but the best French pastries and cakes that damn near float off the plate of their own accord, they're so light.'

Madigan pointed a forefinger and wiggled his thumb above it.

'That's it. Well, Bissom compensated by having a good memory. Better than good – goddamn unbelievable. Could tell you about every battle in the War, when it took place, weather conditions, name of all the regiments that fought, number of casualties, types of guns used, Generals' names, all of that. And not just as recent as the War Between the States – he could go back to the French-Indian Wars, tell you about old coins, all the way back to Roman times...'

'Red Roy Bissom?' Kimble was astounded.

'Yeah. Could've had a good career as some kind of historian or teacher, I reckon. Only he would never have taken it on – he couldn't stand in front of a class with a face like his. First snicker and he'd want to kill 'em all.'

'Sounds like he's wasted his life.'

'Being an outlaw and a killer is his way of getting back at life for what it's done to him.'

'OK. Where does it fit in here?'

'If Jay Sandlo and Mace can't get those chests open, my bet is Bissom is the one who knows the combinations.'

'Why?'

'Because Bissom was with the original armed escort when those chests were being moved to Minneapolis. He was the only survivor and while he didn't know where all the chests were buried, it's my bet he got to know the combinations of those locks.'

Beau Kimble was silent until Madigan crushed out his cigarette against his saddle horn and straightened, getting ready to ride.

'How come you know all this, Bronco?'

Madigan gave him a wry smile. 'I hated every damn minute doing deskwork but to save myself going plumb loco, I read every file that came my way, cover to cover. Jay sent me a really detailed one on Roy Bissom.'

'Almost as if he *wanted* you to catch him?'

'Yeah. But right at the end of the file, he had a big order written in red ink, stood out like a newspaper headline: *Bissom must, at all costs, be apprehended alive!*'

Kimble smiled. 'So he could talk with him. Bronco, you play your cards close to your chest, don't you?'

Madigan arched his eyebrows but didn't answer.

'Let's go, kid. I hope you can remember the way.'

'To each his own, Bronco. Bissom with his dates and numbers. You with your fast draw and "justice will be done at all costs". Me? My speciality is trails and direction. Just follow me.'

It was nearing sundown before the outlaws came in sight of Mace Daggett's hideout. They were weary and irritable, for it had been mighty hot and the thick air was laden with biting insects coming through the heavy timber north of the basin where Daggett holed up.

No one had spoken for a long time – except for Bissom who asked several times when the *hell* they were going to reach this *goddamned* hideaway!

'There!' Mace Daggett growled as they made their way down to the hidden canyon.

When they had negotiated the difficult entrance, Bissom sniffed as he looked around, the shadows deep and dark up around the rise where the outlaws had their lean-tos and what looked like a small cave in the background.

'Not bad.'

'Not bad?' echoed Daggett edgily. 'Better'n any hole in the wall you've ever hid in. Look at that creek. There's a deep-water pool, plenty of fish. We go huntin' in the hills, don't even have to leave the basin if we fancy venison. This is mighty fine, here, Roy. If I was the settlin' kind, I might even think about startin' a ranch.'

Someone laughed at the suggestion but Bissom merely scowled. He glanced at Senator Jay Sandlo.

'You like it, Senator? I mean, it's a far cry from that fancy mansion your wife lets you live in, I guess, but – what you think of it?'

Sandlo gave Bissom a hard look.

'Get your facts right, Roy! That's my mansion. I worked for it.'

'But it's your wife's money that paid for it.'

'I told you to – oh, just shut up! And let's attend to the business in hand.' *End of that conversation – before it even got started.* Touchy! Bissom decided.

As the senator swung down stiffly, Daggett, already dismounted, walked across and placed a hand on his upper arm.

'First things first, Senator. Like where're the chests?' Daggett swung an arm towards the ground close to the remains of the old camp-fire. The last place he had seen those chests.

'Told you. I had Splinter help me hide them.'

191

'Then he met with an "accident",' Bissom cut in, coming across. 'What'd you do? Bury the body?'

The senator's face was hard and ugly: he didn't like being badgered by these outlaws. In fact, he was distinctly uncomfortable with so many of them so close. *If only Madigan hadn't been alerted that things weren't what they seemed! Yes, he would feel a hell of a lot better if only Madigan was still on-side ... ready to help him.*

He had backed himself into a corner now: it had been his intention to come here with just Bissom and maybe one of his men to get the chests out of their hiding-place and open them. He could take care of two men, even a mean cuss like Bissom who would be alerted and ready to make sure there was no double cross, but...

'Where'd you put Splinter, Senator?' Daggett gritted.

Splinter had been one of his best men.

'He fell in the creek and drowned. Couldn't swim. I tried to reach him. I can even show you the long sapling I cut with my knife but by the time I got back he'd disappeared. I guess he drowned.'

'*Fell* in, you say?'

'Yes. Look, I'm sorry. There was nothing I

could do.'

'What was he doin' close enough to the creek to fall in?' asked Daggett.

'Trying to catch a fish, I expect. There was a fishing-pole floating in the creek when I rushed up after hearing him cry out.'

'Senator – Splinter didn't like fish. He was strictly a beefsteak man, preferred it to venison, even.'

Sandlo spread his hands.

'That's all I can tell you, Mace. I tried to save him but – he drowned.'

'Or had some help doin' it,' Daggett growled but before the senator could protest, Bissom said:

'You know what I think happened, Mace? I think the senator and Splinter carried the chests up there and dropped 'em in that deep pool you were talkin' about. Dropped Splinter in, too, maybe...'

'Now, just a minute, Roy!'

Mace Daggett cut in harshly:

'That's likely the way it was. Well, Splinter's gone, whatever happened.' His voice took on a ragged edge. 'Now we want to know where the chests are, Senator.'

The outlaw dropped a hand to his gun butt and all of the faces that watched Sandlo were grim and cold-eyed.

'All right,' the senator said, resignedly. 'The chests are in the pool. There're ropes attached to them, the ends to pull on are hidden under grass on the bank.'

It was the best part of an hour before they had the iron-bound chests, streaming water, out on the bank, the outlaws breathing heavily, wet and short-tempered. Bissom knelt before the chests quickly, ran his hand along the edge of the locks, picked up a handful of grass and wiped them off, crouching closer.

'What're you looking for?' asked Sandlo tightly.

Bissom smiled thinly.

'See these nicks on the cover of the lock? Made with a file. Six on this one, and I reckon there'll be five on the other.'

Jay Sandlo smiled. 'Chests numbers five and six!'

Bissom nodded without looking away from the senator.

'Inside should be directions how to find three and four – and in *those* will be directions for locating one and two. Reckon we're gonna be rich, rich, rich, boys!'

'That's why I didn't want to use dynamite. In case it destroyed the directions to where the other chests are buried,' Sandlo said quietly.

Daggett asked the question uppermost in all their minds:

'Can you open 'em, Roy?'

Bissom looked thoughtful.

'Maybe. Just tryin' to recollect the numbers for these two. Yeah! Think I've got it.' He examined the locks again. 'Might need a little oil – and some light. Get a fire goin', some-one.'

'I saw some gun-oil in the cave,' Sandlo said.

'Go get it then!' snapped Daggett. 'You been standin' round lettin' us do all the damn work haulin' up them heavy chests.'

The senator frowned, not liking being ordered around by this outlaw. But he stood and started back across the ground towards the dark maw of the cave.

'We might's well drag 'em across to where you been making your camp-fire,' said Bissom.

They set about dragging the heavy chests, hitching the ropes to the patient horses, Senator Sandlo starting up the small rise towards the cave.

Breathing a little heavily, he paused just outside the cave, watching the others a moment. Then he turned, ducked his head and went inside, reaching into his vest pocket for a vesta.

'Never mind the light, Jay. Just come in and keep your hands where I can see 'em.'

The senator almost had a heart attack as he recognized Madigan's voice coming out of the darkness. He stumbled and then Beau Kimble had his arm and dragged him deeper into the cave.

'My God! *Two* ghosts!'

'What're they doing out there, Jay?' Madigan asked, and the senator caught the faint gleam of gunmetal in the man's hand.

'Getting ready to open the chests. I was right – Roy Bissom does remember the combinations.' There was no answer and, his eyes growing more used to the darkness now, he made out the two lawmen. 'They caught me in the hills, knew I couldn't've moved the chests far and made me come back here and show them. I was stalling, came here for some gun-oil I said I knew of. For the locks...'

'Was this what you were really after, Senator?' asked Kimbie and held up two twin-barrelled Ithaca twelve-gauge shot-guns. 'Found them wrapped in blankets and buried under the grub supply. You could easily have taken care of that group outside once you had them, Senator. Except for Bissom, of course.'

Jay Sandlo was silent for a moment and then said:

'Well, Roy'll listen to a deal. He opens the chests, one for him, one for me. No need to share with Mace and the others.' He paused. 'I don't suppose you gents would be interested...? No, of course not. I should know better than to ask you, Bronco, and as you've trained Beau as your sidekick ... well, looks like the next move is yours.'

The outlaws were still struggling to drag the chests across to the fire outside. Madigan came away from the cave entrance and asked Sandlo:

'Just what's behind all this, Jay?'

The senator sighed.

'I need money, Bronco. That bitch of a wife of mine has put everything in her name. She caught me in a rather – compromising position with a younger lady and – well, you know what they say about a woman scorned. She kicked me out without a penny. Oh, I have my senator's pay, but I'm used to living way beyond that. And I have debts that must be paid or... Well, I thought I saw a way out, knowing as I did the schedules of the railroads and when they shipped valuables.

But I knew it would be only a matter of time before someone like you would work out where Mace was getting his information.'

'We had our notions, Jay, but I couldn't believe it of you. Should've moved on you long ago, I guess, but...'

'Thank you for your trust, Bronco. Well, it didn't work out and I'm sure Daggett was short-changing me anyway. I couldn't believe it when they dug up these chests of Confederate gold bars. It was the answer I needed. I knew Bissom could still remember the combinations but didn't know how to reach him and get him on side. Then I thought of you and your reputation. If anyone could track him down it would be you–'

'And you put that big red notice on his file that he was to be captured alive...' cut in Madigan. 'But you shouldn't've tried to kill Beau. That was your big mistake.'

Sandlo sighed. 'I know – I – just didn't see that I could handle two of you: you really had trained him well, Bronco. So when we came to that flooded river, I thought I saw a chance of getting rid of Beau and–'

'We can work out the rest...'

'Senator!' bellowed a voice from outside. 'What the hell're you doin' in there?'

'Daggett's getting impatient,' Sandlo said as Madigan edged to the cave entrance. 'He'll send someone up to see what's keeping me.'

'Yeah. Might as well get this over and done with,' Madigan said. He brought up his rifle and fired all in one smooth motion.

Oakes was winding up the rope that had been used to drag the heavy chests across to the fire, the others gathering kindling while one man crouched to get it started. But it was Oakes who took the bullet meant for Daggett.

He stumbled on one end of the rope he was winding around his arm and then jerked and spun as Madigan's slug clipped his shoulder. He fell against Daggett and both men went down so that Madigan's fast second shot passed overhead.

The gunshot had scattered the men and Madigan swore, tracking the rolling, scrabbling Oakes, and firing as the man rose to his knees, clawing at his bleeding shoulder. This time the bullet took him in the head and he was flung violently into Daggett who was just rising, too. The outlaw kicked away from the dead man, shooting wildly across his body, snaking in behind one of the chests. Madigan's bullets whined off the metal casing and then Kimble's Mannlicher opened up beside him. Hood was running for cover behind some rocks and his left leg kicked violently out to one side. Even as he went down, screaming with the pain of a shattered hip, Kimble fired again and the man somersaulted, skidded, and was still.

Bullets chipped the cave entrance and then a shotgun roared, almost deafening the marshals. Daggett reared back, clawing at his face as the charge of buckshot screeched across the metal chest, burning across his scalp and filling his eyes with warm blood.

Madigan brought him down, then swung the rifle hard, knocking the shotgun from the senator's grip. Jay Sandlo grunted in pain and shock, fell. Madigan clipped him with the butt of his rifle.

'Stay out of this, Jay!' he snapped dropping flat as bullets suddenly ricocheted around the cave.

'Stay down, Bronco!' yelled Kimble who was lying prone now. 'Bissom and that other man have found out they can bounce their lead around in here!'

He clawed at the earth as more bullets howled and slashed and thudded around the cave. The men hugged the ground trying to force their bodies into the hard earth. Madigan grunted as a flattened slug cut across his back, slashing his jacket and finding enough of his flesh to draw hot blood.

Kimble rolled deeper into the cave, into the back where the roof sloped down. He cried out.

'I'm hit!'

'Get outta there!' snapped Madigan as he lost his hat, ears ringing. 'Back there's the worst place!'

Another volley drowned anything else he might have said and then he caught a movement out of the corner of his eye, spun on to his side, saw Jay Sandlo picking up the second shotgun.

Madigan dragged his rifle around one-handed but he was too close to the wall. The barrel jarred against a protruding rock and slipped from his hand. Jay reared up, a tight grin of triumph on his face, as he lifted the shotgun.

Madigan reacted instinctively. He hurled himself to the right as the Ithaca came up and there was a thundering roar that filled his head. Whistling balls from the charge of buckshot slapped at his loose jacket but didn't penetrate deeply enough to reach his flesh. He hit the ground rolling, got jammed halfway by the sloping roof. There was just enough room to bring his Colt around as

Jay Sandlo, on one knee now, lifted the shotgun for the final shot.

Madigan dived forward, headlong, gun out in front, triggering. The senator went over backwards and the shotgun discharged, bringing down dirt and stones from the roof. Almost totally deaf now, Madigan kicked away from the wall far enough so he could rise to his knees – in time to find Bissom and Riley charging up the slope to the cave entrance, shooting their sixguns now that their rifles were empty.

Madigan triggered at Riley, saw the man stagger. The lawman threw himself down, firing his last bullet. It knocked Riley back and sent him rolling down the slope. As his hammer fell on an empty chamber, Madigan heard a distant voice yelling, 'Watch out, Bronco!'

He twisted and glimpsed the senator bringing up a pistol that he had likely been carrying under his coat, and which Madigan knew – too late now! – that he should have searched for as soon as he got the drop on Jay. Bissom fired, twice, and his bullets knocked the senator down. Then Kimble's Mannlicher made its snake-whip crack and Roy Bissom's red face exploded like a dropped melon as the powerful bullet took him through the nose.

Madigan fell to his knees, looked around and saw the kid sagging back, blood on his face, smoking rifle falling from his grip even as his eyes closed and he slumped in that tight little corner of the cave.

Making sure there was no more threat from outside as he shucked fresh cartridges from his belt, Madigan reloaded his Colt and crawled back towards Kimble. As he did so, a hand clawed at his jacket and he looked around sharply. The senator was gasping for breath, mouth working.

'Bronco – I–'

Madigan slapped the hand away.

'Got nothing to say to you, Jay. Just lie there and die.'

The words may not have reached Jay Sandlo, as he slumped, murmuring unintelligibly, head resting on his outstretched arm. Then he seemed to sag inwards and was still.

Madigan moved away and reached out for Kimble, shaking him roughly.

'You with us, Beau?'

Kimble's head lolled limply. His eyes remained closed. Madigan shook him again, at the same time trying to see where the kid was hit. Some buckshot had got him in the body but there were a couple of bullet holes and torn places on his jacket, too.

'Damn you, Beau! Didn't I teach you better than to crawl into the back of a cave when someone's shooting into it? You damn fool! Now you've got yourself killed – and I'll have a dozen damn reports to make out and Parminter'll have my scalp. Why the hell couldn't you've just drowned in that river and be done with it?'

'Be – because I thought – you might – need me to – to save your miserable – hide.'

Madigan started at the sound of Beau's voice. The kid's eyes fluttered open and he stared up at Madigan, face twisted in pain.

'I wish – now I – I had – drowned...' Beau gasped.

'Ah, you'll be all right. You've got plenty of miles to ride yet. Might even end up in Parminter's job one day.'

'Don't want – it. Rather be your – sidekick.'

Madigan looked down at him and there was a faint smile on his lips.

'Yeah? Well, no accounting for taste, is there.'

'You're hard – Bronco. You know that? Hard.'

Madigan was fumbling at the kid's clothes and Beau groaned.

'Easy, Bronco! That – hurts!'

204

'Quit being such a sissy. You gotta learn not to moan and groan at every little gunshot wound.'

'How – how many times've I been – hit?'

Madigan seemed to be counting. 'Looks like about nine or ten buckshot wounds – not too serious – and couple bullet holes.'

'That adds up to – a *little* gunshot wound?'

'Long as you're still breathing, it does.'

He wasn't sure but he thought the kid cussed. Then Beau asked suddenly:

'How – how we gonna open the – chests now?'

'Chisels, blow-torch, maybe even dynamite. It's not a big problem. We've got men in the Marshals who specialize in such things.'

'I didn't – know.'

'Well, you've got a lot to learn yet. But keep on as you're going.' Almost as an afterthought, he added:

'You've done OK so far.'

Despite all the pain and the faintness from loss of blood, Beaumont T. Kimble managed to grin.

So far... That sounded good to him.

It meant he was still Madigan's sidekick. Maybe he had a long way to go yet, but Beaumont T. Kimble knew he would make it.

'Just shows how little Doc knows.'

'Bren, I knew you'd react like this. Believe me, it'll help young Kimble and you'll benefit from the extra time here. You're so damn close to breaking through on those railroad robberies I don't *want* to take you off. For any reason.'

Madigan left with a scowl and relations between him and the chief marshal had been strained ever since. He had felt angry enough – and even petty enough, in retrospect – to throw all his research into a pile, gather it up and lock it away in the bottom of a filing cabinet. He dithered around his office corner, tidying up here and there, mostly un-necessarily, snapping at anyone who came in, ignoring messages from everyone up to Parminter himself. A couple of days of this and he realized he was being a fool. An *angry* fool but still, essentially, a fool.

With only minimal reluctance he dug out the railroad files and started going through the information he had already gathered, starting at the beginning. It led him to a name he remembered from some years ago – Mace Daggett, who had made a career of robbing trains and had been jailed for twenty years.

Now he picked up an item he had skipped,

missed, on an earlier reading of a file from the sheriff in Lockwood, Colorado. It had mentioned the sheriff leading a posse on the trail of three escapees from Canyon City penitentiary. Daggett's name was amongst the runaways; he hadn't noticed it earlier.

Daggett had been an expert at his job and had even earned his living hiring out to other gangs, helping to plan their hold-ups and getaways. One of the men he had worked with was Red Roy Bissom, a tough man and one of the most notorious train robbers of them all. He was prime suspect in the spate of hold-ups and derailments that was plaguing the Sierra and Northline Railroad at this time.

Bad enough for the company to ask official help from the Marshals Service. Now Jay Sandlo had bought into it personally. The pressure was mounting.

Madigan knew that Daggett had a brother who lived in Washington and who had been in plenty of trouble with the local law, mostly for assault-type crimes. But he was a hardened criminal and Madigan figured he would likely be in touch with Mace, who had never been recaptured and was still at large, though no one knew where. But Larry Daggett would know.

So Madigan went looking. He knew that to find Larry he would have to go into the toughest part of Washington city. They called it the Ambush Zone, where anyone suspected of having more than a dollar in his pockets could and would be jumped and rolled for whatever possessions he was carrying.

This would be a test to show if he was fit enough to take to fieldwork again. Or it might put him out of action – permanently.

He decided he *had* to find out which.

He was known, of course. He might work undercover out in the field but around Washington he was Bronco Madigan, US marshal, a man it was best not to tangle with. He limped just a little and his shoulders and ribs were still sore but he had given himself several brutal work-outs, tapering off to a regular, more reasonable series of exercises – including guns and hand-to-hand. Doc Rudd had advised him not to go on with such physical exercise at this time but after hours at a desk each day he *needed* such self-imposed exertion. Not that he admitted or allowed anyone to see his distress, but it knocked the hell out of him at first and he was hard put to walk away upright, casually wiping the sweat from his face and scarred upper body, even, once, working up a tune to whistle. *He had sweated every goddamn note.* Just to look casual.

Then, one memorable day something kicked in and he suddenly began to get the rhythm. Everything went much more smoothly, his breathing co-ordinating with muscles, and he began to feel better, even to look forward to what he had been regarding as pure, stupid torture.

Rudd refused to grade him simply because Madigan had ignored his advice to cut down on the physical stuff. So to hell with Doctor Ferguson Rudd. Tonight was going to be the real test.

He was wearing his sixgun although the city police frowned on such things. But he was in the Ambush Zone now and that was a world of its own with its own rules – which were, 'No Rules'. If there was any trouble within the limits of the zone no one sent for the police: it was settled one way or another on the spot – or maybe later with a hired assassin. But the law was never recognized.

The place was called the Wolf Den, which seemed appropriate to Madigan as he pushed in through the battered doors which were loose on their hinges and showed several bullet-splintered scars. There was some sort of music playing beyond the fug of tobacco smoke and for those who could recognize it, a whiff of opium coming from somewhere in the rear. Amongst the notes of the tinny piano and a lazy-sounding guitar, Madigan heard the thin sound of a woman's voice singing something that might have been a toned-down trail ditty.

It was worse than some places he had seen in wide-open trail towns. Through the haze he saw a faded sign over the bar: *Come to Washington and raise a family. Come to the Den and raise Hell!*

Madigan figured he would accept the invitation. When he was eventually served at the bar and sipped the rotgut whiskey he called the 'keep back.

'What d'you call this?' he asked, indicating his glass.

The 'keep was a man with no neck, beefy shoulders and face so battered that Madigan instinctively knew this man would not hesitate to fight anyone or anything at any time, simply because there was no way he could be marked up any worse than he already was. He picked up the glass, held it up to the smoky light, sniffed and set it down again with a nod.

'Aw, yeah. That's our vintage stuff.

Panther's Piss, we call it. Best in the house.'

'Then you drink it.'

Madigan grabbed him by the soiled collarless shirt, twisted so his knuckles were against the man's larynx and spun the man's upper body across the bar, his back straining against the inner edge. With his free hand the marshal poured the whiskey in the general direction of the man's mouth. Some went up the nostrils of the broken nose and the man howled and bucked and choked, sneezing. Madigan rapped his head hard on the bar and released his hold. The 'keep slid over the bar and out of sight, gagging and hawking.

Men around Madigan had snatched their drinks so they wouldn't be knocked over; they looked hard at the lawman now.

'You're fools for drinking this slop,' he said aloud and the two closest men moved in fast: no one called them fools for any reason.

Fists thudded against flesh, other men were jostled. Madigan ducked a wild swing at his head, snatched up a bottle from the bar and smashed it across the head of one of the men as he moved in. He slashed with the broken remains at the second man, who jumped back with a startled yell, held out his hands as he backed off.

'Whoa! Take it easy, feller! You're right

about the stuff they serve here – it is slop. And we're stupid for drinkin' it... OK?'

Madigan hurled the broken bottle-neck aside, curled a lip at the man and spun quickly as someone called a warning and he heard pounding boots. The crowd scattered and two trees came charging in – at least, that was Madigan's impression of two massively built men, one with a nail-studded billy and the other with a sawn-off shotgun.

He shot the man with the gun first, in the beefy thigh, and, as the man yelled and collapsed to the floor, dodged the first blow with the club. It chewed a splintered arc out of the edge of the bar. Madigan rammed his smoking gun barrel against the bouncer's right shoulder and dropped the hammer. The shot was muffled but its impact blew the man back three feet. He screamed as his collar-bone and scapula shattered. The club fell to the floor and Madigan scooped it up, slammed it across the head of the other bouncer who was bringing his weapon around. Madigan didn't even look at the damage he caused the man; he turned and raised the club threateningly as the barkeep came up from behind the counter with a sixgun. The man's eyes widened and he let the gun fall, lifting his hands slightly and backing up against the shelves where bottles and glasses jiggled.

Madigan grabbed one of his hands and yanked the man across the bar, holding the wrist tightly, splaying the fingers against the countertop. He touched the hand lightly with the nails of the club.

'Larry Daggett. First answer had better be right or you're gonna have to have that hand amputated, it'll be in such a mess when I get through with it.'

'Jesus Christ!' the barkeep breathed, struggling. 'He's in the opium room.'

'Show me.' Madigan had the club in one hand, the Colt in the other.

The barkeep nodded and the crowd opened up to let the marshal through on his side of the bar. He paced the whimpering barkeep until they both cleared the counter and then he rammed the sixgun's barrel against the man's back.

'No code – no signals.'

'I – I have to use a special knock or they – won't open the – door.'

'Use it, then. But be ready to die if you get it wrong.'

'Hell, why you pickin' on me? I only work here–'

'You do what I say and you've got a bright

future. Try anything smart and I won't kill you, but I'll leave you crippled for life.'

'Christ, Madigan! I don't deserve this!'

'Here's the door. Give your signal.'

The 'keep didn't hesitate, rapped out his short code, and in a few moments there was the sound of rattling bolts and the door opened six inches. Madigan caught a whiff of the smoke and it stung his eyes, but he saw the doorman's face, sweaty, pale, eyes like gun barrels.

'He wants to see Larry,' the barman croaked.

The deadly eyes moved from the 'keep to Madigan. The voice was not much more than a whisper.

'He's got company – two of them new Chinee gals. Come back in a couple hours.'

Madigan gun-whipped the barkeep to his knees, enough to keep him from starting anything, and kicked the door back. It smashed into the man on the far side, sending him reeling. Madigan stepped in quickly, took time to snap the bolt across on the inside and spun back as the whispering man came up off the floor, blade-steel glinting.

The marshal stepped to one side and the knife buried itself two inches in the door. The man had trouble pulling it free and

61

Madigan backhanded him with the gun across the narrow face. He stumbled to his knees, howling, blood trickling between his clawed fingers.

Beyond, Madigan glimpsed the rows of curtained bunks and a couple of mats on the floor where drugged men and women cavorted in various stages of undress. No one was interested in him or the doorman; the opium they had smoked had transported them to a much better world, one of colours and slow-motion life, delights beyond the common man's imagination.

Madigan hauled up the dazed doorman by his arm, shook him roughly.

'Let's see what kinda show Larry's putting on. Unless you want the base of your spine blown out...?'

'He'll kill – me.' The whisper contained a lot of genuine fear.

'He doesn't, I will. Not a good night for you, friend. *Move!*'

The man, holding a kerchief against his bloody face, led the way to a row of narrow doors down one side to the rear of the building. He opened the second from the end.

Madigan pushed him inside, following and closing the door behind him. He could hardly breathe, the air was so thick with opium and incense and some kind of perfume.

Larry Daggett was on a mattress on the floor with two women, sleek ivory bodies squirming all over the naked man, murmuring and chuckling with musical sounds. Larry was moaning, not even aware of the small audience.

The doorman was down on his knees again, swaying, still dazed and bleeding. Madigan pushed him aside, stepped forward, lifted one startled Chinese girl away from Daggett and placed his now cold sixgun barrel against the man's groin.

Everything froze – sound, movement, even the heavy breathing. Daggett blinked and Madigan leaned forward so the man could see his face. But he kept his gun tight against the man's swiftly withering flesh and said with a cold smile,

'Howdy, Larry. Got your attention?'

CHAPTER 5

OMAHA

It had been a long boring journey north and west from Washington. Though Kimble had to admit that parts of it had suited him well enough.

Like travelling in what passed for luxury on these railroads, the standard dropping little by little the further west they travelled. He had hoped the senator would have a private car but he learned quickly enough that Jay Sandlo was more down to earth than that. He booked a compartment for the pair of them but they ate in the regular dining-car mostly, although Jay did order off-menu dishes, giving Kimble his choice, too, paying extra for the privilege of having the 'chef' prepare the special orders.

'Don't use the tax-payers' money for frivolous things like private cars, Beau,' the senator told him over the first meal on board the train from Washington to Columbus, Ohio. 'But I do like a good meal – good

65

booze, too, within reason. You like wine? Cognac with your coffee?'

Beau returned the steady, enquiring look.

'I don't drink, Senator. Plain soda water'll be fine.'

Sandlo looked steadily at the young marshal, then slowly lit a cigar taken from a gold-rimmed case he kept in his jacket pocket.

'First marshal I've ever met who didn't like his red-eye...'

'Don't like the taste and – well, I used to have a few,' the kid admitted slowly. 'But – I like to keep control.'

Sandlo arched his eyebrows. He didn't comment, but he wondered about that story of Kimble's having to get out of Virginia one jump ahead of shotgun-carrying kinfolk of an unnamed young woman whose honour had been breached. Could be this kid had a few more surprises in store for him.

The journey dragged on, day after day, the senator working on a lot of papers in his bulging valise. Sandlo noted that Kimble merely sat looking out of the window or got up and walked back through the cars as far as he could go, then walked forward as far he could. Taking some exercise, or getting the kinks out.

'You don't read books?' the senator asked over the evening meal served in their compartment as the weather was growing a little colder now.

'Read plenty,' Beau Kimble said.

'Mr Dickens?'

'Yes.'

'Sam Clemens...?'

'You mean Mark Twain? Yes, I've scanned his stuff. Like his satires better than his so-called novels.'

'I was born in Missouri. Know that Big Muddy well. He captured its atmosphere and the people exactly.'

'Well, takes all tastes.'

And that was the end of what Sandlo had hoped would be an interesting discussion.

At Omaha the long journey was taking its toll and the senator announced that they would take some time here to do a little hunting. Red deer had big sets of antlers up this way and he wanted a new set for his den wall back home.

'A match for the ones I've got, near as I can manage it,' he added.

Kimble seemed keen enough. They hired a guide and were taken to country the man said was crawling with red deer, giant stags on every rock, almost.

He was bragging, trying to earn a big fee, and while Jay Sandlo did shoot two deer, their antlers were no more than average. The senator paid off the guide and Kimble said he would track down a suitable stag, just leave everything to him.

Sandlo was a mite put out about the way the kid took over but he figured it wouldn't hurt to give him a shot at it. Parminter had claimed Kimble was a good tracker.

And he was. He passed up two sets of tracks that the senator thought would get him the trophy he wanted, led Sandlo on a gruelling day of climbing up and sliding down steep slopes and, right on sundown spotted the quarry. A huge stag trumpeting as he stood against the glowing sky on a jutting rock. Sandlo was out of the saddle promptly, taking his Remington breech-loader rifle with the brass tube of the telescopic sight glinting like gold.

The senator couldn't find a comfortable shooting position and was still settling when he heard a faint metallic sliding sound, a click – and then the lashing crack of Kimble's Mannlicher. The stag lurched, its delicate feet making a little slithering dance, then it crashed on to its side, head lolling over the edge of the rock.

Jay Sandlo rolled on to his back, eyes blazing.

'What in the *hell* do you think you're doing?'

Kimble looked genuinely surprised.

'He was about to break. He'd done all the calling he aimed to and he was getting ready to break and get back under cover. You weren't yet settled and I figured rather than lose him...'

Senator Jay Sandlo stood slowly, muscles knotted along his jaw, his eyes narrowed.

'I *have* lost him. D'you think I'd put those antlers on *my* den wall when I didn't shoot the animal they belonged to? Goddamn you, Kimble!'

Beau still seemed surprised.

'Well, when my father took me hunting, if an animal looked like getting away and the shooter wasn't ready, whoever was ready took the shot. I'm sorry, Senator, I just thought...'

Sandlo made an effort to control his anger, and nodded curtly.

'You've got a lot to learn yet, kid,' he said.

Next night, after they had gone back to Omaha, Jay Sandlo said, his words clipped:

'I'm going out to eat. Find someplace else and maybe a little female company.'

Kimble sensed the man was still mad at him, asked tentatively if the senator wanted him to come along.

Sandlo smiled faintly.

'You might think I'm not moving in fast enough on the young lady and move in yourself.'

Kimble flushed. 'The hell with you, Senator.'

Sandlo's grin widened. 'They told me you didn't cuss.'

'Only when I'm really riled.'

'I'm learning more and more about you, Beau. Maybe you'd like to go back to Washington?'

'Maybe I would. But I can't. I'm assigned to you.'

'I can change that. In fact, I'll give it some thought. We'll talk about it in the morning.'

He went out and Kimble steamed for a spell, went into the hotel dining-room and picked fault with the meal they served, leaving it only half-eaten as he stormed out after reducing the waitress to tears.

It was cold on the streets of Omaha, a bitter wind blowing, and few people were about. Kimble went into a bar to get warm, started to ask for his soda water, changed his mind and ordered a whiskey. He stared at the glass of brown liquor for a long time before he picked it up. It was six months since he had taken a forced cure at his father's insistence. He had never really gotten over the craving for alcohol but had made the effort when his father had held out joining the Marshals Service as an incentive.

'Stay sober, and I'll have a few words with my old Ranger pard, Miles Parminter, Beau. Get you into the Service like you've always wanted...'

And safe from the father and brothers of that damn Virginia gal...

He tossed down the drink, shuddered, ordered another. Then changed his mind.

'Bring the bottle!' he snapped shakily.

Parminter was hunched over his desk, holding a small oblong of yellow paper, when the door opened and Madigan came in.

He looked brighter than usual, but his face still had a strained look. Still, he moved easily enough as he kicked out a chair and dropped into it, lifting his right leg across his left and hanging his hat on the bent knee.

'Got some news, chief,' he began but the look on Parminter's face slowed him down some. Wondering what might be wrong, the chief marshal spoke before Madigan could say any more.

'I think I might've already heard it.'

Oh-oh!

Madigan waited quietly now. It took only a moment before Parminter continued.

'Understand there was hell to pay in the Ambush Zone last night – in the Wolf's Den specifically.' The cold eyes bored into Madigan. 'Couple of men beaten up, both in the infirmary, barkeep partially blinded by his own rotgut – and some sort of disturbance in their opium room, which, as you know, is tolerated by the city police so that they at least know where the drugs are in town. Two illegal Asian women found – and a man who had severe injuries to his genitals.'

Madigan frowned, shaking his head slowly.

'They say them Chinee women are something fierce once they get aroused.'

Parminter almost smiled. Almost...

'They say it was an off-duty marshal who caused all this. Lucky for ... whoever it was that he didn't try to make it an official visit. Or there'd be hell to pay and I'd have to conduct an investigation and give a full a report to the city police. As it is, I've managed to stall them by insisting that if it was a member of the Service, *off-duty*, and just out for a night on the town...' He spread his hands. 'The Den is notorious as a blood-house and I couldn't really understand why all the fuss.'

'I agree with you, chief.'

'I thought you would. Seems that the police were getting ready to make their own raid on the opium room – as they do from time to time – and their plans were some-what upset. But they managed to find enough of the drug for a conviction of the Den's owners, so it'll all blow over. As long as they're convinced we weren't stepping outside our jurisdiction.'

'Well, that's good to know, chief. I've got some more good news...'

'*More?* You think I enjoyed the fast-talking and shuffling about I had to do to keep the city police from laying an official com-plaint?'

'No, but as long as you quietened 'em down...'

Madigan figured he'd better not pursue this; Parminter could still discipline him severely and that was the last thing he wanted now, so he continued swiftly while the chief marshal was still drawing in breath.

'Chief, I'm pretty sure now that we can prove that Mace Daggett is behind most of

73

these railroad robberies. And if we can get to him and do that, I reckon he'll lead us straight to Bissom. He might even deal to save his own neck. They're distant kin, you know, cousins or something, the Daggetts and the Bissoms. Tennessee renegades.'

Parminter was watching him with a narrow look.

'You say you're *pretty* sure about the connection...?'

'Certain-sure in my own mind. Larry Daggett was in no mood for lying by the time I convinced him he ought to tell me where big brother Mace was and...' He stopped at the stony look on Parminter's face.

'Now there's a coincidence. It was Larry Daggett who had all those injuries to his genitals.'

Madigan arched his eyebrows.

'Yeah? Well, now I come to think of it he was kinda – busy – with a couple of Chinee gals when I first saw him. Didn't say anything to me about his pecker being bruised or that–'

'Funny. His penis was bruised and his testicles had been badly twisted and there were cigarette burns...'

Madigan was shaking his head. 'Well, once or twice I've fancied a Chinee, but this has

74

put me right off.'

'All right, Bren,' Parminter said resignedly. 'Can you depend on what Daggett told you?'

'Damn right, chief. He would've admitted to just about anything.'

'That's what I mean – was he just telling you what he thought you wanted to hear so as to stop his – ordeal?'

'Well, I dunno anything about any "ordeal", but, no – it was gospel.'

'And he told you where to find Mace Daggett?'

'Yeah. He's somewhere around the Nightshades, north of Omaha, and operating as far as Deadwood in the Dakotas.'

Parminter sat back in his chair, took out two cigars and tossed one to Madigan. They lit up and half-filled the office with aromatic smoke before either spoke again. It was Parminter who commented:

'Just the area Senator Sandlo was heading in to. I wish to hell he'd told me why he was going up there. I'm sure he was following some sort of lead, but you know Jay. He likes to do things for himself and he wouldn't involve any law agency that had to be paid for out of the public purse if he wasn't certain-sure of his information.'

'Yeah, I know Jay, all right. And that's just

what he'd do. Take a single lawman with him while he looked into things himself.' Madigan hitched forward to the edge of his chair. 'Chief, I'm plenty fit to go out in the field now...'

'What makes you think so? Doc Rudd hasn't assessed you as fit. Unless you can convince *me* – somehow.'

Madigan cursed under his breath. He'd walked into the trap as usual. That damn Parminter! He was expert at manoeuvring a man into places he didn't mean to go. He sighed.

'OK. It was me went into the Ambush Zone last night. You can see I came out of it OK. Had some opposition but – well, here I am. Raring to go.'

'Go where?'

'To Omaha – get on Mace Daggett's trail, find the way to Bissom. He's thumbed his nose at us for a long time, chief.'

That would strike home; Bissom had been a big thorn in Parminter's side for years. Several times they'd almost had him but he'd managed to slip the law on each occasion. Any chance to bring Red Roy Bissom to heel would be gladly jumped at by Parminter.

Madigan *hoped!*

The chief marshal remained silent, flapped

the yellow form he had been holding. He seemed surprised that it was still in his grasp. He looked down at it, reading.

Without glancing up, he said:

'Yes, I think you'd better get up to Omaha as soon as you can, Bren, and move on to Deadwood or anywhere else the Bissom trail leads. And there's an added chore for you to do while you're up there.'

'What's that?' Madigan felt elated at Parminter's permission for him to travel to where the action was. He'd take on anything as an extra as long as he got out of this goddamn office.

'You'll have to try to find Senator Jay Sandlo. I've just received a pretty damn frantic telegram from young Kimble, saying that Jay went out for a meal two nights ago and hasn't been seen since.'

CHAPTER 6

TRACKS

Most times the weather didn't worry Madigan unduly. If it was hot he sweated and drank plenty of water – if it was available. If it was raining he tightened his patched poncho around his throat and hoped not too much water got in and ran down his back. If it was cold, he pulled on his wolfskin-lined canvas jacket, put on an extra pair of socks, used heavier gloves and slept close to his camp-fire. If he was lucky enough to be inside at night, he hunkered down in his bunk under as many bedclothes as he could pile on.

Usually, riding, he sweated or shivered or got wet and it didn't bother him; there was nothing a man could do about the climate. But now, arriving in Omaha, he was already wearing his wolfskin-lined jacket buttoned to his neck and his hands were cold because his heavy gloves were still at the bottom of his warbag.

The bitter winds blew in across the plains and stirred the dust, put dewdrops on the end of his nose, and squeezed tears from his squinted eyes. And this was only fall! He hoped like hell he could get this chore done and be back down south before winter set in up this way.

A couple of years ago he wouldn't have cared one way or the other. He went wherever and whenever the job took him. Now – hell, he felt like a tenderfoot, pining for warmth!

There had been no address on Kimble's wire to Parminter so Madigan had to find out where he and the senator had stayed. Knowing Jay Sandlo, he reckoned the man would pick a good hotel – and pay for it out of his own pocket – and there was no reason to think he wouldn't keep Kimble close by in a room in the same place.

There were three hotels in bustling Omaha that Madigan figured might fit the bill. He struck it lucky at the second, the Flagler. The clerk had to call the manager, not willing to give out such information across the desk, and the man came hurrying out of a back office, pulling on a frock-coat. But when he saw Madigan in his rough travelling clothes he didn't bother buttoning and seemed regretful that he had bothered with the coat at all. He was middle-aged, putting on weight about the waist and his thinning hair was fluffed up to make it look more than it was. He said his name was Mr Cottrell.

Madigan told him what he wanted and Cottrell looked him over once before answering warily:

'Yes, I know Senator Sandlo quite well. He's a guest here, but he hasn't paid his rent for a couple of weeks.'

'He's still here, though?'

'Just why are you enquiring?'

'He's a friend of mine. Is he still here?'

Madigan's looks and his tough voice bothered the manager and he fidgeted with his open coat, eventually starting to button it so as to keep his fingers busy.

'Well, we have kept the room for him but – I'm afraid we haven't seen him for almost two weeks.'

'And his friend? The young ranny, Kimble?'

Cottrell seemed more uneasy than ever at this question.

'Er – Mr Kimble. Yes. He – he was here until recently. In fact, he got himself into a little trouble and spent some time in jail. I'd recommend you ask Sheriff Duane about him.'

Madigan didn't like the sound of that but knew he wasn't going to get much more out of this pompous manager who was thinking only of the Flagler's reputation. He found the law office and Sheriff Ned Duane turned out to be a sour, lanky man about his own age, but watery-eyed and with blue and red veins showing in his nose, which had been battered to starboard on his gaunt face.

'Kimble? No, never had no prisoner named Kimble. When was this?'

'Not sure – within the last couple of weeks. He was travelling with Senator Sandlo.'

Duane sighed. 'All I know about that one is he went out for supper, which he had with one of our fair ladies in the Blue Star restaurant and then disappeared.'

While he was talking he was leafing through a ledger or record book on his desk. He stopped at a page, ran a finger down a list.

'Had a feller about the time you're talkin' about got a few under his belt and turned nasty and busted up some of the bar in the Hotspur saloon on Sioux Street. Offered to pay afterward but I kept him in jail a couple days. To cool him off and show him he couldn't come into my town and cut loose his curly wolf without payin' for it.'

'Kimble?'

Duane looked at the book again, looked up, eyes narrowed.

'Gave his name as Madigan. Brendan Madigan.'

The Hotspur barkeep seemed willing enough to talk about the brawl started by the tall young ranny with the fancy clothes, especially after Madigan bought him a drink.

'His clothes didn't look so fancy by the time he left,' the man said. He whistled softly and shook his head slowly. 'Come in and was all polite, wouldn'ta thought butter'd melt in his mouth. But he bothered me, you know ... soon's I saw him down that first drink.'

'How come?'

'The way he stared at it a while before he tossed it down. Like a man used to be a drunk and was havin' his first taste in a l-o-n-g time. Then he ordered a whole bottle and I started clearin' the shelves of the good glasses and bonded whiskey.'

'He turn mean?'

'Mean and riled. Mind, I think he was riled at himself, likely for fallin' off the wagon. I've seen it before. I had one of the gals smooch him some, thinkin' mebbe all

83

he needed was a woman. Took her a long time but she got him up to her room.' He sipped some more of his top-shelf whiskey and shook his head again.

'Christ, he was more on the prod than ever when he came back – feller bumped him and that was it. Kid picked him up and threw him half-way across the room. Landed on a table where a few of the railroad boys were playin' a friendly hand of poker. They din' appreciate it. Feller broke the table an' knocked 'em seven ways to Sunday...'

'They beat up on the kid?'

'You kiddin'? Hell, these were hard boys in from the railroad and they moved in on him, but drunk or not, he just wasn't where they threw their punches or tried to kick him. He put down all four and when my bouncer tried to pull him off he knocked him on his ass, too – with a chair. Then for good measure...' He paused and gestured over his shoulder at the shattered mirror and two sagging shelves.

'Threw the chair at your mirror, huh?'

'And picked off six bottles with his goddamn Colt. Took the necks clear off 'em, neat as you please. By that time Duane had arrived with a shotgun. When the kid fired his sixth shot, Duane moved in with two deputies and they cornered the kid – who was kinda tuckered by now, you know – and bent the shotgun over his head...'

Madigan bought the man another drink.

'Friend of yours?' the barkeep asked.

'Not if he uses my name when they jail him.'

The 'keep whistled softly, looking Madigan up and down.

'You look like you can handle yourself.'

'This gal still around? The one the kid went upstairs with?'

The barman looked around the smoky room.

'Don't see her – either got a customer or she's takin' a rest. She won't be able to tell you nothin', but – you wanner wait?'

Madigan shook his head, finished his drink, paid the 'keep and left. He went to the Blue Star restaurant one block back from Sioux on Quarter Street. It was in a neat line of buildings: wig and hat-maker, a barber's shop, shoe-store, bakery at the far end (called the Blue Star Bakery so likely had some connection with the restaurant), an accountant and the office of the town newspaper, Omaha *Clarion*. There was a print shop attached to the rear of the newspaper building. A pretty quiet corner of town for a classy restaurant.

Madigan figured any woman Jay Sandlo had supper with would be a cut above the kind who hung out in the Hotspur: the Blue Star likely wouldn't give him the time of day....

He was mistaken. The owners were proud to have had a Washington senator dine there and they gladly gave him the name of the 'hostess' who had supper with him.

'Mrs Fern Pascale. You understand she is a widow woman, of course, well-versed in the niceties, shall we say, of dinner entertainment.'

Madigan didn't like the sneering man.

'How about the niceties of after-dinner entertainment?'

The man's smiled dropped like a lead sinker and it took his jaw with it for a few moments. Then his mouth clamped.

'No need for that! In any case, I know nothing about what happened when they retired to Mrs Pascale's room. Her business entirely and I rather resent your innuendo—'

'Guess I know Jay Sandlo better than you do. Mrs Pascale in?' The man gave him a withering look and Madigan added: 'If I have to go looking, I will. Knock on every door, kick like hell if I don't get an answer...'

'I tell you only to avoid disturbing our clientele. Room thirty-two. But I warn you, the moment you start up those stairs, I'm sending for Sheriff Duane.'

'I think he might be expecting you,' Madigan said, heading for the stairway in one corner of the restaurant.

The owner was wringing his hands but punched a bell and a man came running. By the time Madigan had reached the top of the stairs the man was hurrying to get Duane.

The woman who opened the door of Room 32 was 'mature', about forty, Madigan judged. She was nice-looking, her figure beginning to spread some now, and she was wearing a silk kimono, her light-brown hair piled on top of her head.

She had nice eyes, blue-grey, but they narrowed now and he saw the calculating glint. She smiled, but it wasn't the best smile he had ever seen.

'Mrs Pascale? The manager sent me up. My name's Madigan. I'm a friend of Senator Sandlo's.'

For an instant there was a blind that closed down behind her eyes, then her smile widened and she stood aside to let him in. He caught a whiff of lavender as he passed her and maybe she moved a little too quickly to close the door, for her sleek hip brushed against Madigan.

He smiled faintly. 'Nice perfume.'

'It's in the soap I use. I've just had a bath.' Her eyes crinkled as she looked him up and down and added: 'Perhaps if you'd arrived a few minutes earlier you could have – scrubbed my back.'

'Yeah, I've had some experience at that.'

'I'm sure. Take a seat please and tell me what you want to know about dear Jay.'

He sat on the edge of a padded chair with a dark, polished-wood frame and a spade-shaped backrest. It wasn't very comfortable.

'He's disappeared. You must be one of the last people to have seen him, if not *the* last.'

She frowned.

'I wondered why he didn't come back. He said he would and I took him for a gentleman and was quite disappointed when he never showed up.'

'You didn't know he hasn't been seen for some time now? Far as I know, he never returned to his room at the Flagler after having supper with you.'

'I – was disappointed that he didn't come back, but I – well, I have my pride, Mr Madigan. It's beneath my dignity to chase any man. I'm sorry. I can't help you.'

This Large Print Book, for people
who cannot read normal print,
is published under the auspices of

THE ULVERSCROFT FOUNDATION

MADIGAN'S SIDEKICK

l ls c

The long, hard years of being an active US marshal were catching up with Bronco Madigan. Scarred and battered, he had to admit that he was slowing down. He almost died in a hail of bullets because he overlooked one simple fact. Worse still his rescuer was a greenhorn and trainee marshal, Beaumont T. Kimble. Wealthy and pampered, with a rich father to pull him out of trouble, Kimble was young and aimed to go all the way. At any cost. He was just the kind of sidekick Madigan needed – like a bullet in the back!

MADIGAN'S SIDEKICK

by

Hank J. Kirby

Dales Large Print Books
Long Preston, North Yorkshire,
BD23 4ND, England.

British Library Cataloguing in Publication Data.

Kirby, Hank J.
    Madigan's sidekick.

    A catalogue record of this book is
    available from the British Library

    ISBN 1-84262-404-0 pbk

First published in Great Britain 2004 by Robert Hale Limited

Published in Large Print 2005 by arrangement with
Robert Hale Ltd.

Dales Large Print is an imprint of Library Magna Books Ltd.

Printed and bound in Great Britain by
T.J. (International) Ltd., Cornwall, PL28 8RW

CHAPTER 1

MISJUDGEMENT

Madigan had faced greater odds than these and walked away from the dead man, so this deal seemed like an easy chore.

It was three to one now – four to one a few miles ago – and he was close enough to see where they were going, yet far enough back to be able to stay hidden.

He *knew* where they were headed, anyway. There was only one place high up here in the sierras that they could or would make for this late in the day. It had to be the old stage station at Signal Rock, a place Madigan had used in the past to overnight, either on a manhunt or crossing the range before heading down to Fort Magill.

He also had the advantage of knowing the lay-out of the only building left in a reasonable state of repair after some drunken travellers had set fire to the main station sheds and outbuildings a few years back.

Madigan was weary as hell. It had been a

long trail across the desert and into the foothills after this wild bunch had pulled the bullion robbery down in Fatigue Creek, killing the Wells Fargo agent and one of his helpers, leaving the other crippled after riding him down on the way out. They also shot a townswoman whom they likely mistook for a lawman as she tried to get to the sheriff's office either for safety or to raise the alarm. The light was bad because of the heavy rain but the buckshot found its way to the woman and killed her right on the doorstep of the law building.

Along the way the gang had raped a rancher's wife and left the man wounded. He had been able to tell Madigan which direction the killers had taken and had asked why was a US marshal on the case of a gang of outlaws who only robbed banks and Wells Fargo agencies.

'It's more than just plain lawlessness,' Madigan had told the rancher. 'They murdered a whole stagecoach full of people up in Lincolnville last August. One of those men was a US Marshal on assignment.' He paused as the wounded man nodded and then gave him a sharp look. Madigan nodded slightly. 'Yeah. He was a friend of mine.'

'Wish you luck. If you catch up with the

big bastard with the red beard, shoot his pecker off before you kill him! He's the one raped my wife.'

Well, there hadn't been time for any fancy shooting when Madigan had managed to corner the red-bearded man on a bluff over-looking the roaring green-and-white waters of the Two Dog River where it surged through the narrow break in the range, like soda gushing from a shaken bottle.

Red Shandon was separated from the others, whether by design or accident Madigan wasn't sure, but he didn't aim to look a gift-horse in the mouth when he spotted the big outlaw riding lonesome up the twisting trail of the bluff.

The tracks of the others skirted the bluff, taking the easier but longer trail around the base and through a series of ravines that gradually climbed higher like a set of giant steps.

'Red's gonna use the bluff for a lookout, see if he can spot me,' Madigan murmured. Talking to himself seemed to be a growing habit these days. He had always done some of it, more thinking aloud than anything else, but now and again lately he had caught himself framing an answer aloud, too. He swore under his breath: just another sign

7

that the years were creeping up on him, he allowed.

But he knew he was right: the only other reason Red would make that muscle-wrenching climb with a near-jaded horse was to set up an ambush. Madigan was too much of an old hand to ride into a headshot or backshot from a prepared ambush to fall for anything like that. Shandon would know it, for they had tangled several times over the years. Maybe they even respected each other – a little.

Madigan's dun mount was tired and he changed to his spare, a hardy little grulla with a slit in one nostril left long ago by a Comanche arrowhead. The dun was content to follow on the lead rope without saddle and rider, although Madigan had left the saddlebags and warbag slung on the horse's back. It made things a mite easier for the grulla and it would be able to reach speed just a fraction faster than if it was carrying full load. Enough time to make the difference between stopping a bullet and dodging it.

The marshal misjudged Red Shandon, though. The man set up an ambush of sorts, but didn't aim for the lawman – he shot the grulla out from under Madigan and would

have got the dun, too, if it hadn't baulked on a bend, wrenched the lead rope from the rider's hands and backed up out of sight of the rifleman.

Madigan just saved himself from going over the edge. The grulla went down fast, forelegs folding, the rider tilting abruptly over the bending head and shoulders. But Madigan had taken front falls from a dying horse before and knew they were the most dangerous: a man usually sustained more head and chest and shoulder injuries that way than if he took a tumble sideways. So Madigan instinctively threw himself to the left, towards the edge of the trail above the roaring river. He twisted in mid-air, hearing the rifle uptrail blasting in a hurried volley, his boots kicking at the low rock that jutted out over the river. The impact jarred through his body, clear up into his skull, and he threw himself on to the side away from Red Shandon.

It put him on a narrow ledge of rock, a hundred feet above the gushing Two Dog – and there was little room to spare. Ricocheting bullets spattered him with rock dust as he squirmed closer, trying to force his body *into* the damn rock. Sweat rolled into his eyes as he brought the rifle around awk-

wardly, the butt scraping over the granite.

Red thought he had him, stood up with a triumphant yell that was choked back into his throat as Madigan sighted coolly through the hail of lead with which the outlaw raked the rock, and squeezed off his shot. Red Shandon wrenched back, twisting. Madigan heard his grunt of pain as he fell out of sight, put another shot into the brush up there, low down. He was pretty sure he heard the slap of lead into flesh again but it could have been just the bullet clipping the brushwood.

Funny – Madigan didn't think he would have hit Red with that first shot, but figured it would go close enough to upset his aim. Anyway, Red was down and hurting by all counts. His gun was silent, and Madigan was still stretched out on about ten inches of flat rock overhanging the powerful flood of water far below.

He began to ease back to the trail. The dun whickered but had enough sense not to show itself around the bend. The grulla lay bleeding and still, tongue lolling, eyes wide, a hungry crow already circling against the hot sky. Madigan moved slowly, carefully, scarcely breathing, expecting Red Shandon to open up again as soon as he crawled away from the rock on to the narrow trail.

10

Red might have been hit but he was far from being dead. He waited until Madigan got clear of the rock, enough to hunch up with safety and crawl back on to the trail. Then he reared up from behind the bush, rifle hammering as he worked lever and trigger.

Bullets splattered all round Madigan's fast-moving figure as he hurled himself downtrail, rolling for the bend, knowing the risk he was taking. If he misjudged his speed he would fail to make the bend and would slide out into space.

Red Shandon must have emptied the rifle's magazine but although his lead came mighty close none of the bullets struck Madigan and he rolled and skidded wildly into the bend. He snatched at solid rock with his free hand and there was a pause, a brief hiatus in sound and motion, and he heard the lever on Red's rifle clashing repeatedly, the click as the hammer fell time after time on an empty breech.

Madigan dug in with his heel, feeling pain shoot up his calf into his groin, but it stopped his wild slide and he rose to his knees, rifle blurring to his shoulder. He raked the brush, leaves and twigs erupted and Red Shandon gave a grunting yell, thrashed, and his rifle

skidded down the trail.

He was down, hit hard this time, and Madigan reloaded his own weapon, turned and lunged at the trailing rope of the dun. He didn't aim for it to run off downtrail and leave him stranded up here with a wounded killer above him.

But he heard one final groaning, half-yell, a crashing of brush. He looked back around the bend in time to see Red's body hurtling off the trail, spinning over and over before it fell into the tortured water with a barely visible splash, whipped away by the wild currents in seconds.

So much for any more threat from Red Shandon.

He found the man's horse tethered to a sapling above the bloody patch of ground behind the brush where Red had lain in ambush. The animal was really tuckered-out and Madigan didn't have the heart to use it. He off-saddled the horse, noting a badly worn cinch-strap and turned it loose. There were no saddlebags or warbags.

He whistled softly, shaking his head.

'Not like Red to trust the others with the loot, unless they stashed it somewhere along the way and I missed it. Guess maybe Red was growing old, too. He sure was a worse

shot than I remember. Well, he won't grow any older.'

Madigan mounted the reluctant dun and set off over the bluff, seeing the distant abandoned buildings of the old way station.

It would be a couple of hours yet before the others reached it but there was no doubt in his mind that that was their destination. *Man, he was tired!* And his knee hurt and his back ached where he had wrenched it while holding himself on that slab of rock above the river.

With luck he could move in on the other three outlaws, get the jump on them, and then use one of the old bunks or a bedroll to stretch out on for a good night's sleep.

He figured he had earned it. Or would have, after he'd nailed the outlaws. There was no thought about taking them in for trial; it would be hell getting any survivors out of this country and they would have to go all the way back to Fatigue Creek, anyway. So he had already decided: there would be no prisoners. Only justice, dished out by a blazing gun.

His blazing gun.

He gave them time to settle in, get a fire going in the rusted but still serviceable old

pot-bellied stove in what had been the passengers' rooms, then he moved in. Slowly. Warily. Smelling charred bacon and burnt cornpone.

Twice a man came to the door; he thought it was the one called Coley. The second time the man said, with a note of worry in his voice:

'Red oughta be showin' by now if he nailed that marshal.'

'You know Red,' a voice from inside said. 'Devious bastard. Could be creepin' up here to finish us all off so's he'd have all the gold for himself.'

There was laughter from inside but Coley said:

'That better not be so!'

'Relax, Coley. Only joshin'. Red's OK. Hell, he's made us all rich. C'mon. Let's drink to wild trails an' wilder women! May there be plenty of both!'

Madigan heard the clink of bottle and glasses then; he figured now was the time to move in.

The marshal closed in on the door and kicked it open, stumbling as more pain shot up his leg. It *would* be the one with the bad knee which he used!

But he glimpsed the three of them sitting

14

around a table covered with plates and bottles – and guns. He worked rifle lever and trigger as he dodged to one side, Coley snatched a shotgun from the table top and whirled. Madigan's lead struck the man but didn't put him down. He staggered and swung the Greener in a wild arc, triggering. The big gun jumped out of the man's hands and Madigan, rolling on the uneven floorboards now, braced the rifle butt against his hip and put two bullets into Coley which slammed him back on to the table.

His body knocked a carbine out of the hand of a black-bearded outlaw who swore as he pushed the already falling Coley away. The other man, short, bald, but wearing a tobacco-stained frontier moustache, came round with two sixguns blazing.

Madigan twisted, his rifle barrel striking the edge of the heavy table, throwing his shot and almost tearing the weapon from his grip. He was under one end of the table now. He heaved up with a roar, up-ending it, hand streaking for his sixgun. He nailed the bald man through the face as the black-bearded man brought up his own Colt, blazing. The marshal stumbled backwards as lead tore across his left upper arm and another bullet jerked at the loose cloth of his

15

shirt. He continued his spin all the way around, corkscrewing down to one knee, chopping his hand at the gun hammer.

The three shots sounded like a burst from a Gatling gun and Blackbeard was flung back into the hot pot-bellied stove, but made no sound as his body slowly slipped to the floor, his shirt bloody and singed.

Ears ringing, nostrils and throat raw with the thick gunsmoke, Madigan climbed slowly to his feet, wincing as he put weight on his right leg. *That blamed knee!*

He had thumbed home two fresh shells into the Colt's chamber when he felt a blow smash into his body, driving him violently into the wall. He fell and twisted as he did so, seeing a man standing in the doorway with a smoking pistol in his hand. He didn't recognize him in the dim glow of the lanterns but he could plainly see the murder in his eyes.

'So you're Madigan. Well, this was your last trail, Marshal. But I thank you for killin' the others. Now the bullion's all mine. You can die knowin' you done me a good turn–'

'Drop your gun!'

Both men jumped at the sound of the voice coming from the darkness behind the would-be killer in the doorway. He spun

around, sixgun arcing.

'Drop it and lift your hands! You're under arrest!'

'Not this time!' the man growled and fired twice.

At the same time Madigan lifted his own sixgun and triggered. The killer jerked to his toes, started to turn. Madigan put his last shot into him and then fell back in a sitting position, shoulders against the wall, legs splayed.

The would-be killer was down, twitching briefly before he went still. Madigan tried to thumb another cartridge into his gun but his fingers were numb and he fumbled, dropped the brass shell. He was working at freeing another from the belt loop when the doorway was filled by another figure, a tall young man, clasping a bloody hand low down on his right side.

His face wasn't clear but Madigan, his sight fading fast, saw the mouth work and dimly heard the words, finally recognizing the newcomer.

'Hey! You shot him in the back!' the man gasped, accusingly.

'Oh, hell! Not Beaumont T. Kimble!' Madigan moaned and passed out.

CHAPTER 2

ON THE MAT

'Good grief, Bren! He saved your life!'

Chief United States Marshal Miles Parminter's truculent voice reached just beyond the closed door of his Washington office and a couple of the clerks and researchers, busy at their desks outside, glanced up, wondering if Marshal Bren 'Bronco' Madigan was once again on the mat.

Inside, Madigan, looking grey and drawn, his wolflike face leaner than ever, set those disturbing grey-green eyes on his boss's hard face.

'Or did I save his life?' he said quietly.

Parminter frowned, snatched his cigar from where it rested on the edge of the metal ashtray and puffed rapidly, shrouding his face in aromatic smoke. A sure sign he was irritated.

'All right. Let's say you both helped each other stay alive when you shot down Lansing. In the back.'

19

Madigan nodded.

'Sure, I'll go along with that, chief, Lansing shot me, and Kimble's arrival grabbed his attention, and I shot Lansing but he wounded Kimble first. Sounds complicated as hell but I guess that's about the strength of what happened.'

'It's exactly what happened according to Beau's report – *and* your own.'

Madigan leaned back in his chair, wincing a little as pain coursed through his battered body.

'Well, how come you're yelling at me?'

Parminter was about to yell that he *wasn't* yelling at him for Chris'sakes, but threw a rope on his rising anger and forced himself to relax. He stabbed out his cigar, rose and crossed to a battered sideboy where he poured two stiff bourbons. He handed one to Madigan, his piercing grey eyes almost the same colour as the cropped hair covering his bullet head in a fine cap. He sniffed, straightened his wrinkled, eroded face and lifted his glass.

'To the end of the Lansing Bunch.'

Madigan hesitated briefly, drank, and watched as his boss went back behind his desk and dropped into the chair.

'So that's why you've got a burr under

your saddle. Lansing.'

Parminter's eyes narrowed and he sipped a little more bourbon before answering.

'Bren, you've been my top operative for more years than I care to remember–'

'*You* care to remember!'

'Don't interrupt, damnit! You've been the best man I've had – still are. But – you're slowing down.'

Damn it! Madigan thought. He had no answer to that. He was now – what? – forty-two, forty-three years old, but he had taken a hell of a beating these past ten years in the Marshals Service. Nine bullet holes in his hide. Three or four broken bones. Two splintered stone arrowheads still flushing somewhere in his veins. He'd been whipped once, and another time he'd been caned with a sapling, had several concussions, walked with a permanent, slight limp from where a man who had been trying to kill him had ridden him down with a horse that stood seventeen hands high.

Yeah – he would concede he was slowing down some. He was a mite more cautious these days, that was damn sure. But he always completed his assignments and had never turned in a negative report.

He admitted these thoughts aloud and

Parminter nodded impatiently.

'I know that, Bren. You're still top man, as I said. But ... this was a close one, you have to admit. Lansing nearly got you. If it hadn't been for young Beau...'

'Well, he did have an advantage. He knew about Lansing. I never knew the man existed.'

Parminter leaned forward across his desk.

'That's my point. You slipped up, went after the gang.'

'And the bullion – as per your orders.'

Parminter's mouth tightened.

'My orders, as always, were loose enough to allow you plenty of discretion in their execution. And you should have picked up on the fact that Red Shandon, while being rat-smart and a killer, *didn't have the brains to plan all those robberies and pull them off successfully!*'

Madigan held up his right hand, spreading the fingers.

''Five. Five raids on Wells Fargo depots or stages and Red's gang got away each time. Till the last. Why would I think he didn't have the brains?'

'Well – why *did* you think he had?' the chief marshal countered. Madigan realized he was in real trouble here.

He eased himself in his chair but still sprawled awkwardly because of the slow healing of his back wound.

'Hell, chief, I just told you. Every raid he pulled he got away with it. By being ruthless, not leaving witnesses who could or would talk, planned his getaway trails and only lost two men in seven months. Took us damn near that long to find the connection back to Shandon himself.'

'And you missed something while you were doing that. You were *looking for* that connection for so long that when you found just a hint that you were headed in the right direction, you overlooked something else.'

Madigan's gut tightened. By God, the old feller could be right! He had done mental handsprings when he had first made the tenuous link between those two dead outlaws and Shandon and Wells Fargo. They had both been drivers or shotgun guards way back. They would have known routes and schedules, which wouldn't change too drastically, and, in fact, were changed almost to schedule, too. Three weeks on the mining run, say, north of the Pecos, then two to the same destination but using the Salt Fork trail, and two weeks crossing the mesquite. *Then back to the mining run again – and so on.*

A pendulum. A *regular* pendulum....

Hell, a seven-year-old kid could work out just which trail the stages would be taking weeks in advance, and that gave the clue as to which depot safe the cash would be kept in.

He looked up slowly at Parminter.

'What did I miss?'

'You missed Lansing.'

'How?'

'Told you. You were too eager to make the connection between those dead outlaws and Red Shandon. But they weren't the ones giving him the depots or the stage trails. It was a man *still working for Wells Fargo*.'

Madigan felt himself tighten all over.

'Lansing?'

'Of course. Barrett Lansing, chief express officer of Wells Fargo at Denver, where all routes for the stages are approved.'

'Hell, he must've been making good money. Why the hell would he tie in with someone like Red Shandon? A bloody-handed killer and thief who'd spent more than half his life in jails.'

Parminter snorted.

'Money, why else? *Big* money, several years' salary in one strike. You look at their raids and you'll see that each time the loot got bigger and bigger, like they were testing

themselves, working their way up to the big one, which was...'

'The bullion haul at Fatigue Creek,' Madigan said, with self-anger giving his words a bitter edge. 'How much was there? Twenty-thousand? Thereabouts?'

'Closer to thirty. Yes, that's what Lansing wanted. He knew the big haul was coming, where and when. He passed the information along to Red Shandon and they pulled it off. You ever stop to think it was just a mite *too* easy the way you got on to the trail Red's bunch was using for their escape route?'

Madigan had. He *had* felt it was just a little too smooth and easy but – hell, by then he was near tuckered-out. He grabbed at the information he'd bought from the half-breed scout at the army post on the Lavender Creek reservation and hit the trail.

'We figure Lansing had it all worked out. He knew you and what you were capable of. He set you on their trail, ordered Red to bushwhack you – if successful. I guess Lansing would have finished Red anyway. But he planned his move around your beating Red, closing in on the others and wiping them out in your usual efficient manner.'

Madigan snapped his head up at the tone in the chief's voice.

25

'It's been OK with you for a long time, my *efficient* manner!'

Parminter waved a big hand.

'He used you to wipe out the gang, which left him all the bullion for himself. And he almost succeeded.'

Bronco Madigan had been thinking rapidly these past few minutes; his eyes had taken on the look of bullets protruding from a sixgun's cylinder.

'You set that kid on Lansing's trail?'

Parminter smiled and Madigan knew he had asked exactly the question the chief marshal had been waiting for.

He shook his large, bullet-shaped head.

'No, Bren. It was Beaumont T. Kimble who worked out Red Shandon's information had to come from higher up than an ex-driver and shotgun guard. He pin-pointed Lansing. I'll admit at first I was sceptical, as he was still a trainee, but I gave him a little rope and, sure enough, Lansing took some unscheduled leave prior to the bullion robbery, time enough for him to get down to Texas and meet up with Red and his men. Or to kill them all and keep the bullion haul for himself.'

'Kimble figured that out...?'

Parminter smiled faintly.

'Pretty damn good for a trainee, eh?'

'Yeah, it is. And you're right, chief, I shouldn't've missed it.'

The chief marshal was silent, looked expectant, but Madigan said no more.

'I gave him the OK to go in and warn you that Lansing was in the picture. He was held up when his horse was bitten by a snake but he used his head, walked ten miles to a small ranch, stole a mount and rode like hell to that old staging station – where he saved your neck.'

Madigan pursed his lips.

'Well, I've had a month to think about it and I consider myself mighty lucky.'

'And so you should. Beau–'

Madigan held up a hand.

'Not because of what Kimble did, but because he did anything at all.'

'What does that mean?'

'I saved his neck, too, chief, no matter what you may think. If I hadn't nailed Lansing, admittedly distracted by the kid, Kimble would be dead. Me, too maybe. But the first thing he said coming into that room was: "You shot him in the *back*." Now you tell me if that sounds like the making of a good marshal.'

Parminter held his gaze.

27

'He's young, still got ideals, but he's top of his group in just about every field, Bren.'

'Just about...'

'All right. He's good with gun and rope and knife and survival, tracking, riding, brain power...'

'But...'

Parminter sighed. 'He does have a tendency to want to give everyone an even break. Very nice if it would work, but we know the way it is and his future would look mighty grim if he was allowed to run around with that kind of notion.'

'Hell, he wouldn't have any future...'

Parminter nodded again, he was openly smiling now.

'No. He needs training, hard training, in that category. By someone who really knows the ropes.'

He stopped speaking and Madigan looked up, waiting for him to continue, but Parminter only kept staring at him, still smiling.

Then he felt the coldness surge through him and he sat up straight in the chair, ignoring the pain it cost him.

'*No!* Goddamnit, chief, *no!* I'm not going to wet-nurse that kid and wipe his nose for him! I'm not–'

Parminter shrugged, interrupting.

'Well, I didn't think you'd go for it, so as soon as the medical officer OKs your return to work, you report to Research and Records and I'll find someone else to bring Kimble into line.'

Madigan's face was a dirty grey now. His hands gripped the arms of the chair so tightly the fingers were dead white.

'You son of a bitch!' he breathed – not too loud, but he saw that Parminter heard him. 'You blind-sided me!'

The man smiled tolerantly and held out a paper for him.

'It's best if you spend a few months out of the field anyway. You get older it takes just that much longer to recover, don't you agree?'

Madigan made no move to accept the paper, his eyes bleak.

'No – I – don't!'

'Well, Doc Rudd feels that and it's his recommendation in your case, Bren. Of course, I have the right to reject his opinion, but, under the circumstances...'

'*All right.*' Madigan would have heaved to his feet in angry indignation if he could have done so without collapsing immediately afterwards, but the best he could manage was to straighten his shoulders and hold

them in a stiff signal of futile rage.

'Oh? You're willing to give it a go? You'll undertake Beaumont's final training – and then use him as a partner in future operations.'

'Christ! This is getting worse! I don't need any goddamn sidekick!'

'Hmmm. Think it would be better if you tried it for one or two assignments, Bren. Help give Beau confidence, too. Definitely think it would be better...'

Madigan slumped. He was beginning to think it might have been better if Lansing's bullet had done the job properly and finished him off.

CHAPTER 3

BEAU

Beaumont T. Kimble. No one so far had found out what the 'T' stood for and Beau wasn't saying. Madigan figured he was just being childish, for that was how he saw Kimble: still not quite grown up, coming from a well-to-do family (the father some kind of friend to Parminter) and used to plenty of money and easy living.

Legend had it that he *wanted* to be a US marshal, but there was other talk that hinted Beaumont might have had to make a mighty fast decision about where he was going before the irate father and brothers of a young woman in Virginia caught up with him.

As it was well known that anyone stupid enough to kill a marshal – or even try to kill him – was as good as dead themselves the Service seemed to be a pretty smart choice.

Personally, Madigan didn't care how he came to be in the Service, but he wished he

hadn't been landed with him. The kid was pleasant enough, even if there was an irritating amount of cockiness to go with it; only twenty-four years of age and not bad looking, the world was his. But his easy living showed and he looked kind of soft, tall, but wide-shouldered. He had performed well enough in the physical work and outdoor training. He claimed his expertise with guns came from following the sport of target-shooting and hunting. He said once that his father had hired an Indian to teach him tracking and survival in the wilderness. It turned out his father had once been a Texas Ranger with Parminter in the early days before he married into Virginia money. Beau was a good horseman, too, knew some fancy ropework and was eager enough, volunteering for menial jobs that other trainees did their best to avoid. The others bet that wouldn't last long.

Madigan grudgingly admitted – to himself, no one else – that the kid might have some potential.

It was up to him to bring it out.

Then, despite himself, he asked: 'How come you wanted to leave that rich-boy life and join the marshals, kid?'

Kimble looked at him soberly.

'I've wanted to be a US marshal since I was seven years old.'

'Childhood dream, huh?'

'You don't have to say it that way! It was a dream, sure, but I worked at making it a reality.'

Madigan hadn't wanted to get into this but now he seemed to have trapped himself.

'What'd you do? Throw a tantrum till Big Daddy fixed things for you through his old friend Parminter?'

Kimble looked angry. 'What the hell's the matter with you?' The 'hell' told Madigan the kid was really upset. But he said nothing. 'I grew up having a lot of money – or my family did – and it bought us just about anything we wanted. So what? I'm not ashamed of it. I admit I've used the family name and influence over the years – but why shouldn't I?'

'Make your own way in life, kid,' Madigan told him curtly. 'You'll be better off.'

'Like you?'

Madigan was ready to bristle but let it ride.

'Forget I asked–'

'No! I'll tell you why I wanted to be a marshal – because I saw one ride into a bunch of five heavily armed bank robbers

and tackle them without hesitation. He killed them all and was badly wounded himself. I've never forgotten that man's heroics.'

'You say this feller took on *five* outlaws?' Madigan said slowly.

'Five. Right in the main street of Hornswoggle, Texas.'

Madigan frowned. 'What the hell would you be doing in a trash hole like Hornswoggle?'

'I was in a stagecoach with my mother and sister on our way to El Paso and a holiday on a *hacienda* in northern Mexico... The bank-robbers were just coming out of the bank, shooting. I saw a woman and a man fall in the mud–'

'Mud? In Hornswoggle? It's in one of the driest parts of Texas.'

'Yes, but there'd been a cloudburst a couple of days before and the place was a quagmire. The stage was stuck on Main, which is how we found ourselves in the middle of the shootout....'

Madigan suddenly seemed far away as the kid went on speaking. *A stage on the Butterfield run, coated with dust from the roof-rack down to the window-sills, spattered with mud the rest of the way, the wheels sinking into the slush of Main... He had had to wrench hard on*

34

the reins to swing his big buckskin around it as he brought up the sawn-off shotgun and downed the first of the robbers as they hit their saddles, right outside the bank...

The buckskin slid out from under him and his second barrel discharged into the air as he tumbled from the saddle. But he managed to drop the shotgun and snatch his rifle free of the scabbard and when he hit the mud, he slid almost ten feet – towards the bank-robbers.

They were shooting but the marshal was sliding at a good rate and their bullets only plopped and splashed into the slurry. He wrenched on to his side as he slid to a stop, levering, bringing his rifle around. He triggered, got one of the horses. It reared and plunged, crashing into the others as they tried to ride away, causing a wild, chaotic tangle.

The rifle crashed again and again. Another horse reared, screaming and pawing, throwing the rider. One of the robbers got his mount moving and ran it at the prone figure in the muddy street. The lawman fired and levered but the rifle's magazine was empty now. He rolled desperately to one side and, as the horse thundered almost

on top of him, cracked the rifle barrel across its forelegs.

The animal swerved and whickered and the rider swayed wildly, snatching at the reins, missing with the shot he fired at the marshal. By then the lawman was hard to distinguish from the mud slurry, but this swamplike creature surged up to its knees and flame stabbed from the right hand. The outlaw was leaning far out of the saddle to get a good shot in. He took two bullets through the head which sent a pinkish-grey spray into the humid air. The horse wrenched one way, limping, and the body plunged into the street.

The marshal was already moving, slowed down by his burden of slush, but he leapt at a rider racing past, the man with the bags of cash, obviously aiming to make his escape while the lawman was busy with his side-kicks. The marshal dragged the man from the saddle even as the last robber wheeled his mount, jumped down and ran in, kicking. The lawman grunted as the boot slammed into his back. He rolled away from the man he had pulled off the horse, and found the other robber already drawing a bead on him, gun hammer falling. He hurled himself aside but the bullet took him some-

where in the body and he spun, cannoning into the other man who was rising to his feet groggily. The man swung his sixgun wildly and it knocked the lawman's Colt from his grip.

He took another bullet in the left upper arm as he grappled with the man he had pulled from the saddle, causing the second robber to hold his fire. The marshal got behind his man, grabbed his gunhand at the wrist and directed the Colt at the standing outlaw. Pressing the outlaw's trigger finger, he shot the other twice, strained and twisted and got the smoking gun up under the chin of the man he held and force-fired the last shot.

It wasn't pretty but the lawman's mask of mud saved him from some of the gore and, swaying unsteadily, he let the dead man sprawl at his feet. He blinked mud from his eyes, gagging for breath. Then he felt a tug at his trousers. Thinking one of the outlaws must be only wounded, he prepared to kick savagely, and then looked down into the awed, excitement-flushed face of a boy about seven years old.

The kid held up the marshal's own muddy sixgun. 'You dropped this, sir...'

A woman was screaming from the open

door of the stage only feet away. *'Beau! Beau Kimble!* You come back here right this instant!'

That incident had happened just after the only cloudburst in Hornswoggle's history – seventeen years ago – and the one and only time they had ever had mud in the main street. Madigan had been lucky to live through that gunfight for one bullet had seared a lung.

Now he looked at Kimble soberly.

'I remember that shoot-out at Hornswoggle. Never named the marshal, did they? The Service doesn't recognize 'heroics' – if that's what it was. You're paid to do a job: bring in the bad boys or bury 'em where you shoot 'em.'

'Well, I pestered my father until he found out who that marshal was.' Kimble paused, smiling faintly as he said: 'If I'd known that under all that mud you were so damn ugly, I might have changed my hero-worship to someone else.'

'That stuff's for kids,' Madigan growled. 'You ought've grown out of it by now.'

'Oh, I'm growing out of it fast – by the minute. I knew you were tough and a lone wolf, but no one told me you were such an

ornery cuss.'

'Let it go, kid, before it turns into insubordination.'

'Why don't you like me, Bronco?' Kimble sounded genuinely puzzled. 'I saved your life at that old stage station. And I was happy to do it.'

'Well, that's what you were being paid to do – but you were kind of slow. You should've shot Lansing as soon as you saw what was happening.'

'I – didn't want to shoot him in the back. I thought we should try to take him alive.'

'Then you haven't been trained properly, kid. But we'll take care of that – starting right now. Let's see how you shoot. Targets don't shoot back so you ought to be pretty steady with your aim.'

'You think I'm a coward?' Kimble was shaking now.

'We'll find out before we're through. But, no, I don't think that. Like I said, you just need proper training.'

Beau sneered at the Winchester lever-action rifles that were standard issue for the marshals. He preferred to use a bolt-action, seven-shot Mannlicher, hand-made in Germany with heavily chequered stock and

his name in silver wire set into the wooden fore end.

'That fancy stuff won't make it shoot any better,' Madigan told him curtly.

The proof of the fine rifle's ability – and that of the man using it – was on the firing range.

It was a very accurate gun and made a sound that Madigan thought of as a snake-like whipping sound. He wasn't sure just where that allusion had come from but whenever he heard the rifle fire it somehow reminded him of a snake striking. In any case, it made a most distinctive *crack* when Beau pulled the trigger, nothing at all like the booming of the Winchesters. The bolt made less noise than the levers which wore at the pivot-points after a lot of use and sometimes became loose and clattery.

'Bolt's slower to feed the ammo,' Madigan remarked when they were down at the rifle range.

'Not necessarily,' said Beau. He spoke in a young, somewhat superior tone and Madigan figured it was just one more thing that would aggravate the hell out of him. 'Depends on the situation. If I have time, I like to draw a careful bead and hit my man, not just spray bullets all over the countryside.'

'Uh-huh.' Madigan threw up his own battered Winchester, which had just come back from maintenance by the armoury, and pumped five fast shots into the target at a hundred yards. It took about six seconds. The spread of holes around the bull could be covered by a playing-card and every shot would have been lethal on a man's body. Which was pretty damn good given the type of ammunition that was available at the time.

He said nothing but Beau caught the challenge in the older man's eyes and smiled thinly as he braced the butt of the Mannlicher against his hip and began firing, working the bolt back and forth smoothly, cartridge-cases spinning from the ejector port, three in the air at the one time. As the first shell hit the ground, Beau fired the other two rounds and the sound of the big rifle whipped and rolled across the range in the bright sunshine. The spread of the five shots was about the same as Madigan's Winchester, but the gun had been fired from the hip, not the shoulder. Which made it good shooting – damned good shooting.

'Now you've strutted your stuff,' Madigan said a little stiffly, 'see what you can do if you take time to aim properly.'

He knew by Beau's grin that the kid had

41

been just waiting for such an opportunity. He stretched out on the mound, settled the engraved silver butt-plate into his shoulder and adjusted the Vernier-scale sights for windage and distance. It took just over seven seconds for the young trainee marshal to get off all five carefully aimed shots.

They made a single hole, less than an inch in diameter – destroying the bull's eye totally. He rolled on to his right side, released the clip magazine just in front of the rifle's trigger guard and slapped another home.

Then the smile of complacency froze as he felt the warm muzzle of Madigan's Winchester press just under his left ear.

Bang! You're dead.'

Beau frowned and wriggled around so he could look up. The rifle muzzle kept the pressure against his head.

'Why?'

'You had an empty gun in your hands. Anyone could've gotten the drop.'

Beau looked puzzled. 'It only took seconds to slap home a fresh magazine. I'm wearing my sixgun, too, you know.'

'And *lying* on it... You rolled on to your right side. Your body pinned your handgun rig to the ground. Rifle empty. Like I said – *bang!* You're dead.'

Beaumont T. Kimble went very still, his smooth cheeks burning. Then he nodded very slightly.

'Thank you, Bronco. I won't do that again.'

'Good. That's a damn good rifle, all right.'

'It should be. Cost my father over two thousand dollars.'

'All that fancy silver inlay work will get you killed, though. Sun'll flash off it like a mirror.'

Beau frowned down at the lovely inlaid work.

'What can I do about it?'

'Paint it over. Scratch it up so it doesn't shine so much, dig it out of the wood!'

'Oh, now that's going too far!'

Madigan shrugged. 'I can savvy your attachment to the gun. It'd look good on any wall, resting on a set of red-deer antlers, but for work in the field it's not worth a wooden nickel. Either dull it down or get an issue Winchester.'

Beau was still examining his Mannlicher, face kind of sad now. He nodded.

'No thanks. I'll paint it over, I think. I see I've a lot to learn.'

That surprised Madigan but he answered affably enough.

'You have. And if you aim to stay alive, you'll learn your lessons well.'

'Oh, there was never any doubt about that. And now that I'm being tutored by the very best the marshals have to offer...' He broke off when he saw Madigan's face.

'Don't push it, kid. I've been a marshal for more then twenty years and I'm still learning. You stop learning in this game you might as well retire, because it's the only way you'll live long enough to see your pension.'

Beau's face was flushed again as he picked up his fancy buckskin rifle case with the Indian bead-work and painted medicine symbols. He slid the gun home, buckling the flap closed.

'And take that flap off the scabbard. You need to get your rifle out in a hurry, you'll still be fighting those buckles when the first bullet knocks you out of the saddle.'

Beau nodded, took his long-bladed Bowie knife from his hand-tooled leather sheath and cut off the flap.

'See Morrie Cavanaugh back at the barracks,' Madigan told him. 'He'll stitch on some leather straps so you can fix the case on your saddle.'

'If I offer him ten dollars will that be enough?'

Madigan had been turning towards his horse and as he lifted one boot towards a

stirrup, looking hard at the kid.

'Money doesn't buy everything, kid, not here. You can try Morrie with the offer but he might just wrap that rifle-case around your head – without taking the gun out first.'

Beau looked bewildered. 'But I don't expect him to do it for nothing!'

'No. But just keep it in mind he did you the favour and when you see a chance to repay him in kind – do it. You'll win more friends that way than trying to buy them.'

Beau went red and his mouth tightened. For a moment, Madigan thought he was going to cuss – though no one had heard him swear yet – or even take a swing at him. Then he straightened out his face and said quietly:

'I've always had to pay my way. Because I was a Kimble. I – don't know any other way.'

A frown flitted across Madigan's rugged face and for a moment his eyes softened a little. He felt a sudden, unexpected – and unwanted – sympathy for Beaumont T. Kimble. Coming from a rich family had its drawbacks, he guessed.

'Well, you'll learn it's different here, a different world. You need more than brains and plenty of money here. Most of all you need understanding.'

'I – I'm beginning to see that.'

Beau watched Madigan mount, stiffly because of his still-healing wounds, then turned towards his own horse, a fine buckskin – another gift from Kimble Senior.

'One other thing,' Madigan said. 'There won't always be time for you to adjust that Vernier sight. Best get used to snap-shooting. Take a couple of hours and let me know how you do.'

'Snap-shooting?'

'Sure. You don't always have to kill your man outright. Does some of these damn outlaws good to suffer a little. Settles their souls, you might say.'

The advice was delivered deadpan and the kid smiled. He thought he might be just getting a glimpse of the real Madigan now. Just a glimpse. But it was a start.

'Any other advice?'

Madigan thought for a moment.

'Yeah. Never tackle seven men if all you've got is a six-shooter.'

CHAPTER 4

BODYGUARD

Senator Jay Sandlo chuckled as he closed the report file and dropped it on Parminter's desk.

'I'll bet Bronco Madigan had something to say about wet-nursing that Kimble kid! How did you manage to hogtie him long enough to settle him behind a desk?'

'He's not *settled* by a damn sight,' Parminter said, almost growling. 'Not a day goes by I don't have him poking his head around my door telling me how fit he feels and have I got a field assignment for him.'

Sandlo was a big man, late forties, well-groomed but with more of a regular outdoor tan than usual for a Washington-based politician. He wore a trimmed moustache which was liberally sprinkled with silver although there was only a touch of grey at his temples. His hair fell in natural waves and his hands were big, showed old signs that this man had used them in earlier years

for more than pushing a pen or hammering home a point in election speeches.

'Well, I hope he's telling the truth, Miles. I want Bronco riding with me when I head north.'

Parminter sat up straighter in his chair.

'You're going north this time of year? I thought you liked the sun and warmth?'

'That I do, and if I could find a worthwhile job to take me down to Texas or even south of the Border, I would.'

That 'worthwhile' gave a clue to the man; sure, like a lot of his colleagues he could come up with some sort of reason to head south and stay there so as to miss much of the bitter Washington winter, but Jay Sandlo was a man who took his position seriously. He said he had been elected by the people and he aimed to give them their money's-worth. If he was going north, then Parminter knew there would be a damn good reason for it. He tapped a file he had brought with him.

'Aim to look into all those train hold-ups,' the senator said. 'I'm the one that OK'd that railroad route, so I want to see what's going on.'

'I know about the series of train robberies. We're moving on it. But it could be danger-

ous, Jay.'

Sandlo nodded absently. 'It won't be all work – there'll be time for some hunting and a little recreation. That's why I want Bronco. We fought in the same company, the Missouri Loyals under General Jefferson McCall at Gettysburg, the Little Round Top charge, as well as half a dozen other battles. We've kind of kept in touch, painted a few towns red and they tell me this Deadwood where I'm headed is a good place to let loose the curly wolf. Madigan's worked up that way, too, I believe.'

Parminter pursed his lips, nodding gently.

'I've just about gotten him convinced that he's the only man to do research on the railroads. He's got a real knack for it and he's producing good results.'

Sandlo arched his eyebrows.

'But you can spare him for a few weeks, can't you? He could do some on-the-spot investigating.'

Parminter shuffled papers he didn't need to.

'Rather not, Jay. Not just now. There's a deal of pressure on this department over this and other things, as well as the old beef about the marshals dishing out rough justice. I need to let things rest up for a bit.'

'But Bronco's just the man to help me out, Miles. I've got pressure on me, too. Opposition's making much of the fact that I approved that rail route.'

Parminter didn't like being put on a spot – not even by someone as pleasant as Jay Sandlo. His voice hardened just a little.

'Yes, Bren's had plenty of experience, but, like I said, he's making good progress with research. A couple of weeks and we'll have enough to plan our move.'

Sandlo looked sharply at Parminter. 'You're protecting him!'

'The least I can do, Jay. Doc Rudd says some of the lead or arrowheads he's still carrying in his body could possibly start to move and make him permanently desk-bound. Or worse.'

Sandlo sighed. 'Yes, I can see how you'd want to play fair.'

'*He* doesn't think I've been playing fair.'

'I'll bet he doesn't. Well, I still want a marshal with me, Miles. There's a chance that the information I have could lead to something where I need that kind of back-up. I thought I'd just make it look like a tax-payers'-funded trip and use the hunting trips as a cover while I checked things.'

'Young Kimble's done a lot of hunting.'

Sandlo's mouth was open to continue speaking and now his jaw sagged a little.

'You're trying to unload a greenhorn on me?'

'He *was* a greenhorn but Madigan's been training him and – well, you saw his report on Kimble.'

The senator smiled crookedly.

'So that's why you had it all ready for my arrival...'

Parminter shrugged his heavy shoulders. 'Only time we see you is when you want something, Jay, and usually it's to use one of my marshals. Beau could use the experience.'

Sandlo gave it some thought and Parminter, urging, said:

'His father is a mighty keen hunter. He used to take young Beau with him on his trips, hired an Indian to teach him. He even impressed Madigan, though hell'll freeze before you hear Bren admit it.'

Sandlo stared levelly at Parminter for a long moment, then he smiled slowly.

'By God, you're a devious man, aren't you, Miles.'

Parminter spread his hands, looking innocent.

'Just trying to help you out, Jay...'

'*And* yourself!' growled the senator. Then

51

he smiled. 'But – I accept your offer.'

Madigan didn't ordinarily go looking for trouble but he was prepared to make an exception to his self-imposed rule this night. He was in a sleazy part of Washington, was actually doing his job, tracking down someone who kept in touch with everything lawless that went on round the country.

He had been simmering for a couple of weeks now, ever since Parminter had sent off Kimble as bodyguard-companion with Senator Jay Sandlo.

'You're gonna get the kid killed,' he told Parminter curtly. 'He's not experienced enough.'

'He's getting the experience now. Who better to bring him along than Jay Sandlo? You know he's a good man and more the kid's ... social level. Beau needs to have some fieldwork apart from straight crime investigation.'

Madigan's mouth and tone were bitter.

'Would've been just the kind of chore to ease me back into fieldwork.'

Parminter sighed, but his attitude was unbending. 'I go by what Doc Rudd reports and he says you're not ready for active and violent work.'